"Here goes nothing," John said.

Mia hurried over, laid a hand on his shoulder and gave a reassuring squeeze. He glanced up at her, and her blue-eyed gaze was understanding but worried. Despite that, she said, "Whatever it is, we will handle this."

He didn't know if the *we* included him. He wanted it to. He wanted that and more, especially with Mia.

"We will," he said, but it sounded almost robotic, and she clearly picked up on that and more as well.

"It is a *we*, John. We will do this together," Mia stressed.

The slight tightening of her hand coincided with the damning ding.

Peering around at the family members gathered in the conference room, he felt as if he was the executioner on judgment day, but he had no doubt about what his program results now meant for them and for him.

"We're all in danger. Someone is going to end our lives unless we can figure it out."

BISCAYNE BAY BREACH

New York Times Bestselling Author
CARIDAD PIÑEIRO

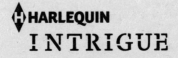

HARLEQUIN®
INTRIGUE™

ISBN-13: 978-1-335-58243-0

Biscayne Bay Breach

Copyright © 2023 by Caridad Piñeiro Scordato

Harlequin Enterprises ULC
22 Adelaide St. West, 41st Floor
Toronto, Ontario M5H 4E3, Canada
www.Harlequin.com

Printed in U.S.A.

New York Times and *USA TODAY* bestselling author **Caridad Piñeiro** is a Jersey girl who just wants to write and is the author of nearly fifty novels and novellas. She loves romance novels, superheroes, TV and cooking. For more information on Caridad and her dark, sexy romantic suspense and paranormal romances, please visit www.caridad.com.

Books by Caridad Piñeiro

Harlequin Intrigue

South Beach Security

Lost in Little Havana
Brickell Avenue Ambush
Biscayne Bay Breach

Cold Case Reopened
Trapping a Terrorist
Decoy Training

Visit the Author Profile page at Harlequin.com.

CAST OF CHARACTERS

Mia Gonzalez—Mia and her cousin Carolina run a successful lifestyle and gossip blog and are invited to every important event in Miami. That lets "the Twins" gather a lot of information about what is happening in Miami to help South Beach Security with their various investigations.

John Wilson—John is a tech genius who recently sold his start-up for millions of dollars. He's building a new tech start-up and trying to develop a personal life out of the limelight that his success has created.

Miles Wilson—Miles is John's older half brother and works with John at his new start-up. He was always protective of John but also jealous of all that John has been able to accomplish.

Ramon Gonzalez III (Trey)—Marine Trey Gonzalez served Miami Beach as an undercover detective before retiring and joining South Beach Security. Trey is the heir apparent to run South Beach Security.

Josefina (Sophie) and Robert Whitaker Jr.—Trey's cousins are genius tech gurus who work at South Beach Security and help the agency with their various investigations.

Ricardo Gonzalez (Ricky)—A trained psychologist, Ricky helps South Beach Security with their domestic abuse cases and other kinds of civil assignments. When he's not working at the agency, Ricky runs a support group for individuals suffering from trauma.

Chapter One

John Wilson's internal alarms were ringing louder than the warning sirens in a nuclear power plant.

Someone had tried to get into the servers, and he had no doubt why: they wanted to steal the new software he was developing, which made him worry for multiple reasons, other than the obvious attempt at theft. First and foremost was that even he had concerns about what this software could do and what would happen if it fell into the wrong hands. Secondly, because it meant either someone inside the company was behind the attempted hack, or had blabbed to someone outside the company about what was supposed to be a top-secret project.

Regardless of the reason, he had to act to protect his code. But he wasn't sure he could do it alone and there was only one group of people he could think of that could help: South Beach Security.

He had no doubt they would assist if he asked since he'd helped them in the past, but involving the Gonzalezes' family-run agency meant having to deal with one prickly and beautiful family member: Mia Gonzalez.

Their relationship, if you could even call it that, had started off clumsily and ended even more awkwardly. Mia and her cousin Carolina, affectionately nicknamed "the Twins," were well-known social-media influencers and also regularly helped the family with their personal and professional connections to gather valuable information for the agency.

Despite that, he knew he had no choice but to call the Gonzalez family for their assistance. This project was just too important to risk.

But first, he had to take steps to make life more difficult for whoever was trying to hack his company. A scan for malware on all the end points and servers; making sure his cybersecurity programs were working properly; checking for any and all targeted attacks; and finally, changing passwords across his different access points in case any of them had been compromised.

"What's up, bro?" his brother, Miles, asked as he strolled into John's temporary office. Since he'd sold off his tech start-up several months earlier, he and the half dozen or so employees who had come with him were in a small, leased space in a Brickell Avenue building, just a couple of blocks down from the South Beach Security offices.

John swiveled in his chair to face Miles. His brother was dressed casually, like so many Miamians. He wore a pale yellow *guayabera* shirt that hung loosely over sharply pressed khakis. His dark blond hair was cut short on the sides, but longer on top, where strands were ruthlessly plastered in place with gel against the Miami heat and humidity.

It made John feel a little—no, make that a lot—underdressed since when he'd rolled out of bed this morning, he'd jerked on one of his many graphic T-shirts and well-worn jeans. As for his hair, he nervously ran his hands through it to tame the rumpled waves.

"Not much," John lied, wary of mentioning his concerns to anyone in the company, even his brother.

Miles narrowed his hazel eyes, which were so much like his own it was like looking into a mirror. Although sometimes John didn't like what he saw. Like now.

"You sure?" Miles pressed.

"I'm sure. Just a little wonkiness with some code I'm trying to figure out. What are you up to today?" John asked, swiveling back and forth in his chair.

"Heading over to the Del Sol to finalize plans for Friday night's party," Miles said as he tucked his hands into his pockets and tottered back and forth on his heels.

John was so done with Miles's party scene, but his brother enjoyed the attention and the women. He suspected that Miles knew that, hence his slightly guarded reaction. But since the parties were important to Miles, he went along with it.

"Sounds good. Do you think they could add some Cubanos to the menu?" He had a hankering for the tasty pork-ham-and-Swiss-cheese sandwiches he'd shared with Mia when they'd gone out a couple of weeks earlier.

Mia, he thought again with a rough sigh. "Do you think the Twins will be coming?"

Miles shrugged and narrowed his gaze again as he said, "I can invite them if you want but I thought you were done with Mia."

He did a little lift of his shoulders and swiveled to and fro in the chair again. "I am. Just wondering is all."

Miles nodded and flicked a finger in the direction of his computer. "Are you sure I can't help?"

Miles was a decent enough programmer, but John wasn't letting anyone near this software project. He

waved him off. "No need. Just doing some routine security checks," he said and nearly bit his lip since it was a
different reason than he'd given before. He hoped Miles
wouldn't pick up on that.

Miles opened his eyes wide. "Someone hacking us?"

He shook his head and waved his hands again. "Like
I said. Routine checks. I'd let you know," he said even
though he wouldn't. He'd already been stung once before when leaks about a problem had made his old company's stock price dive. He suspected someone had done
it intentionally to short the company's stock.

With a quick salute, Miles said, "I guess I'm off to
the Del Sol then. Let me know if you want anything
besides some tasty Cubanas."

"Cubanos," John corrected, uncomfortable with how
Miles was referring to Mia and Carolina, two Cubanas
who would also not appreciate his joke.

"Chill, bro. Just kidding," Miles said with a laugh
and left the office, but John saw he was immediately on
his phone, and he hoped it was just to coordinate with
the hotel about the party.

He hurried to his door, closed it and returned to his
desk. After unlocking his smartphone, he checked it
out to make sure it hadn't been hacked. Satisfied, he dialed Trey Gonzalez, the current second-in-command at
South Beach Security. He'd gotten to know Trey quite
well since he and his fiancée, Roni, had investigated
him about a month ago when John had been a suspect
in one of their cases.

A few weeks after that, right when he'd first started
seeing Mia, he'd also helped Trey with a different case
involving an abusive ex-husband attacking his ex and

bribing building inspectors to ignore dangerous construction issues.

"*Hola*, John. Good to hear from you," Trey said.

John clenched his lips as he said, "I'm not so sure it's a good thing you're hearing from me."

Trey was silent for a moment. "If you need help, we're here. We help our friends."

John was grateful that Trey wasn't doing it solely out of a sense of obligation because John had helped SBS in the past. He'd had few friends in his life, since he was always too busy, first with putting food on the table and later, building his business. But his gut told him that Trey and some of the other Gonzalez family members could actually be friends.

Well, except for Mia, of course. The last thing he wanted was to be in her friend zone.

"Thanks, Trey. I'd like to keep this as quiet as I can," he said, worried that another leak would hurt his new venture.

"Totally understand. Why don't we meet at Versailles at noon? It'll be just two friends having lunch," Trey said.

"I'd appreciate that." John swiped to end the call.

He had several other checks to run so that he could give Trey as much information as he could about the possible hacks during their lunch.

MIA POPPED INTO Trey's office and held up the bag with the *café con leches* and Cuban bread toast she'd picked up at a nearby restaurant to surprise him.

But as she walked in unannounced, it was impossible to miss her brother's brooding look that told her something was up and that it wasn't anything good.

When he saw her, however, he shuttered that worried expression, grinned and clapped his hands. "Please tell me that's breakfast."

"It is, *hermano*," she said, and quickly added, "Everything okay?"

He nodded, tight-lipped. "Totally, how about you? What brings you to the office so bright and early, and without Caro?"

"Carolina is doing a short mom-daughter getaway with *Tia* Elena. I didn't feel like being a third wheel and remembered you still had some things to unpack," she said and gestured to the corner of his office, where a few boxes still lingered.

Trey dipped his head to acknowledge it. "I haven't had a chance with everything that's been going on."

Her older brother had definitely had a lot happening between almost being killed during a police investigation, leaving the department, getting engaged and dealing with a case involving their younger brother, Ricky, and the woman who was now his fiancée, Mariela.

Trey rose and strolled to a small conference table at one side of his office. She followed, laid down the bag and pulled out the breakfast she'd brought. As she did so, her smartphone chirped a message notification.

She pulled out her phone and grimaced as she saw it was from Miles Wilson, inviting her to the Del Sol for a Friday night party.

"You don't look happy," Trey said as he sat at the table, slipped the top off the *café con leche* and took a sip.

She held up the phone for Trey to see. "I gather you're not a fan," he said.

She wrinkled her nose as if she was smelling a dirty

diaper because that's how Miles made her feel. Dirty. "Not a fan at all," she said and sat down to have her coffee and toast, although the text had diminished her appetite.

"Is that why you and John—"

"No, it's not, and when did you become such a gossip?" she teased and elbowed her brother playfully as he sat beside her.

Trey chuckled. "When my *hermanita* starts dating an eccentric multimillionaire tech guru."

"He's not all that eccentric and we were never 'dating,'" she said with air quotes for emphasis.

"You were 'going out.' What happened?" Trey kidded with similar air quotes, but despite his lighthearted tone, she sensed there was more behind his question.

She deflected. "Not much. He was nice. We had fun," she said with a slight lift of her shoulders as she sipped her coffee.

"Sounds…boring," Trey replied and wolfed down a big piece of toast.

Surprisingly it had been anything but boring. Too many men treated her as if she was a piece of arm candy to make them look better. To his credit, John hadn't. He'd been respectful and had seemed genuinely interested in finding out more about her as a person. And there had been some sparks, only…

She didn't enjoy the parties, like the one to which she'd just been invited. Or the flashy red Lamborghini he drove. Those things screamed "lack of confidence," and in her mind, there was nothing sexier in a man than confidence.

Like her brother Trey. He had confidence in spades, which was just what was needed to become the next head of South Beach Security. She asked, "You getting settled? *Papi* okay?"

"Yes, and yes. I know *Mami* and he are happy I left the force. *Papi's* doing what he can to make me feel welcome here, even going business-casual," Trey said as he finished the last of his toast and hungrily eyed the half she hadn't touched.

"Take it," she said and pushed the piece toward him.

As he devoured it, she shook her head and said, "You are never going to fit into your tux for the wedding."

He grinned, a boyish relaxed grin that had rarely happened when he was on the police force. "I'll work it off, don't worry."

She didn't. She had never seen her brother as happy as he was now, working with the family and engaged to Roni Lopez, her closest friend aside from Carolina. It made her heart ache with joy for them, but also hurt a little for herself.

Trey was truly happy with Roni.

Her younger brother, Ricky, was seriously in love with Mariela.

And she was…still busy hitting the social scene with Carolina. Not that she didn't like spending time with her cousin. It's just that lately, with her biological clock inching toward thirty, she wanted more in her life. Someone who would be there for her like Trey and Ricky were for Roni and Mariela.

Maybe even a bigger role in her family's business and not just the occasional help that she and Carolina regularly offered. She had a degree in business administration, after all.

As for John Wilson… He wasn't the kind of guy who could give her what she wanted.

YOU PROBABLY WEREN'T a Miamian if you hadn't eaten at Versailles at some time in your life, John thought as he found a parking spot on *Calle Ocho* near the restaurant. There were a number of people lined up at the take-out window—*La Ventanita*, as it was known to locals. If you wanted to know anything about what was happening in Cuba, Little Havana, Miami, or Washington involving Cubans, all you had to do was hang out around *La Ventanita* to find out.

He hoped the restaurant wouldn't be quite as busy as the take-out window.

John got out of the nondescript BMW sedan. He had thought it better to take that than the flashy red Lamborghini Veneno. While it was an amazing vehicle, he didn't really like calling attention to himself, but Miles thought John had to maintain a certain image in order to attract investors for their new venture.

John thought that if anyone was stupid enough to invest money based on the car someone drove, they were asking to be fleeced.

He walked to the hostess podium to ask for a table, but realized Trey was already sitting at one in a back corner of the restaurant. Trey flagged him down and he excused himself and walked to meet the other man.

"Good to see you, John," Trey said and rose to brohug him.

"Thanks for agreeing to meet me." John took a seat opposite Trey, his back to the crowd of diners. It occurred to him then that Trey had picked the table and John's seat to provide the highest privacy possible in such a public place.

"Anytime," Trey said and picked up his menu to take a look.

John did the same although he knew what he was going to get. He was hooked on Cuban sandwiches and the teeth-achingly sweet shakes the restaurant made.

When the waitress came over, they ordered, and Trey quickly got to business. "You said you needed help."

John hesitated and bit his lip, but then blurted out softly, "I think someone is trying to steal my new software."

"I'm assuming you don't have a clue who is trying to do that," Trey said nonchalantly.

"I don't. I'm running a bunch of scans. I've beefed up security on the servers and supercomputer—"

"Like beefed-up security technology-wise, not like security guards and alarm systems to keep people out?" Trey asked.

The waitress came over with their shakes and placed them on the table. When she stepped away, John said, "We have some security like that. We hired Equinox ages ago, before I knew about SBS."

Trey picked up his glass to take a sip. "They're a good company. I can call and ask what they're doing and, if you don't mind, add anything I feel may be necessary."

John held up a hand in a go-ahead motion. "It's why I'm hiring you."

Trey shook his head. "We owe you for all the help you gave us with Ricky and Mariela. Not to mention not outing Roni during that earlier investigation. Besides, we're friends."

Friends. There was that word again and John wasn't going to argue with him. He needed friends, especially loyal ones like Trey. "I appreciate that."

"No problem. As for the tech side of things, I know you're a smart guy, but Sophie and Robbie are really good at what they do. Would you mind if they helped out?"

So far John had kept any access to his new program to himself and he really wanted to keep it that way. "I'll give them as much access as I can, but my new code… It's really important to keep it secret."

The waitress walked over and placed their sandwiches in front of them and a plate of ripe plantains in the middle of the table. Trey picked up his sandwich and took a big bite. After he swallowed, he nodded and said, "I get it. We'll respect any boundaries you set, but if you don't mind my asking, what exactly does this program do?"

In truth, even John was having trouble defining just that because the program was proving to do so much more than he'd ever imagined it could. He kept it simple because he was sure that he'd have to explain again once he met with Trey's tech-guru cousins. "It's a program that reviews data, finds trends and makes… predictions," he said, hesitant to use a word like that because it created all kinds of expectations in people's minds.

As expected, Trey arched a dark eyebrow. "Predictions. Like who'll win the next Super Bowl and stuff like that?"

"In theory you could, if you fed those stats into the system, but you could also use it to analyze what your competitors are doing, facial recognition, weather, customer churn—"

"What is customer churn?" Trey asked with a puzzled look.

"How many customers you lost during a specific time frame," John said and took a bite of his own sandwich, enjoying the tasty combo of the meat, cheese, pickles and mustard. He chased down the bite of sandwich with the super sweet mango milkshake and smiled.

"Sounds like it can do a lot," Trey said and snagged a ripe plantain from the plate in the middle of the table.

"It can. You can even use it to predict possible crimes and their victims," he explained, which made Trey perk up.

"Really. How does it do that?" he asked, but John waved him off.

"How about you set up a meeting with your cousins and anyone else you think needs to be in on this case. I can tell you more about how the software works, and we can decide what to do to stop whoever is trying to break in."

"I think that sounds like a plan. Can you come by the office in the morning?" Trey asked and, with a slurpy sip, finished the last of his shake. He ordered another one with a shake of the empty glass in the direction of the waitress.

"Diabetes, much?" John joked.

"I know. For some reason, I've had this horrible sweet tooth lately. Hungry, too," he admitted and forked up another sweet plantain.

"Boredom, maybe? I imagine working at SBS is quite different than what you were doing as an undercover detective."

Trey shrugged his broad, muscular shoulders. There wasn't an ounce of flab on them, or anywhere else on Trey, from what John could see. "Different for sure but in a good way. I like spending time with Roni and my family. You know how it is."

"Actually, I don't. My family life, it was kind of dysfunctional so being around you all… It's really different for me," he admitted.

"Sorry to hear that, John. No matter what happened with Mia—"

"Nothing happened with Mia. I respect her too much to treat her like that," he said to shut down whatever Trey was thinking because he did want this man as a friend.

"Glad to hear that," he said and accepted the second shake from the waitress as she brought it over. After a healthy sip, he said, "Mind if I come by on Friday to make sure?"

John narrowed his gaze, not understanding, but when it hit him, he muttered a curse. "Miles. He invited Mia and Caro to the party."

"He did. Let's say Mia was less than pleased," Trey admitted.

"I'm sorry. Miles has his own way of keeping both me and the company in the limelight. You can tell Mia she's free not to come," John said and polished off the last of his sandwich.

Trey laughed heartily. "Tell Mia? Did you forget what my little sister is like?"

John smiled. He hadn't forgotten, which was a big part of his problem with Mia. He just couldn't forget her.

"I'll see you tomorrow," he said and motioned the waitress for the check, but when she came with it, Trey snagged it and tucked several bills into the leather wallet.

"Cash is king, John. Remember that. Until we figure out what's going on, no credit cards. Have you checked your phone to make sure it's clean?" Trey said and handed the waitress the wallet.

"As far as I can tell," he admitted.

"Good. We'll have Sophie and Robbie double-check it tomorrow during the meeting," he said and rose, but when John started to stand, Trey signaled for him to sit.

"Wait a few minutes and then go. No sense risking that anyone sees us together until we have more info on what's happening," he said and, without waiting for a reply, he left.

John sat there, running his straw through the runny remains of his shake. He hungrily eyed the last ripe plantain on the plate before giving in and eating it. Impatient, he looked at his phone and figured it had been at least a few minutes since Trey had left.

He got up and walked out, satisfied that he'd taken the right steps to protect himself and his new software. He hoped that being with the Gonzalez family might give him another chance with Mia.

CLACK, CLACK, CLACK went the fake shutter on his digital camera.

He zoomed in with the telephoto lens to get a better look at the man who had been sitting with Trey Gonzalez, and as he zoomed in, he sucked in a sharp breath.

"John Wilson," he murmured. He recognized the man from some news reports on a recent charity event Wilson's new software company had sponsored.

Interesting, he thought, wondering what the tech multimillionaire had to do with Trey. As far as he knew, it was Mia who had been hanging out with the man. Maybe that's what this little meeting had been about: what Wilson's intentions were toward Mia.

The Gonzalez family was a little old-fashioned that way. They stuck together. Protected their own.

Too bad they hadn't cared at all about what had happened to his family. How his family had suffered over the years while the Gonzalez family had achieved the American Dream.

He intended to make sure that they'd pay for that suffering when the time was right, and his gut told him that would be soon.

He'd been patient after the last attack, waiting for them to let down their guard. It had dropped...a little. That was obvious from what he'd seen of today's lunch meeting.

Trey had done his best to hide in that back corner and not be seen with John Wilson, but he didn't know who he was dealing with. Trey and his family had underestimated the danger for months now, but soon he would give them what they deserved: the same kind of pain and loss he and his family had endured for over sixty years.

Soon, he thought, and snapped off a few more photos.

Chapter Two

When John returned to his office, his brother was there. His feet were up on his desk and the chair was leaning back precariously. Miles was thumbing through the latest issue of a tech magazine, but when he saw John, he casually tossed it on John's desktop and sat up.

"Where have you been, bro? I came to get you for lunch," Miles said, a broad smile on his face.

"I had a...date," he said, wishing he didn't feel so unsure of his own blood, but until he got to the bottom of this, everyone was a suspect.

"That Gonzalez girl again?" Miles asked with the lift of an eyebrow.

"A business lunch," he said but then wished he hadn't.

"Why didn't you ask me to come along?" Miles asked, touchy as always about his role in the business.

With a shrug, and to keep Miles from getting angry, he said, "I didn't think anything would come of it. Just someone trying to talk me into looking at their building for our new office space."

"And?" Miles said and shot out of John's chair.

"No interest. It was in South Beach, but way too small for what we're planning," he said, making sure to emphasize the *we're* when he spoke.

That seemed to mollify Miles a little. With a shrug, he said, "It would be nice to be in South Beach."

Miles loved all the glamour and partying in the area, but John wasn't convinced that was the kind of impression they'd want for potential clients. He favored a location in downtown, like the one they had for the start-up he'd sold, but he didn't say.

"Do you want to do dinner tonight?" he asked, changing the subject to avoid having the same old argument with his brother.

Miles was too smart not to see what he was doing, but didn't challenge him. "I'd like that, bro."

"Great," he said and mentioned one of Miles's favorite places along the Ocean Drive strip in South Beach.

"How does eight sound?" Miles said.

"Sounds good. It'll let me get some more work done on the program," John said, and Miles perked up at the mention of the software.

"Is it going better than this morning?" Miles asked, his sandy-colored eyebrows raised in question.

"Still giving me some issues, but I hope I'll get the kinks out. How are the other projects going?" he said, referring to the apps and programs he'd assigned others to code and which Miles was supposed to be overseeing.

"Okay. We should have more for you to look at soon."

"Great. We'll need those projects bringing in money until I can do more on this program," he said and jerked a thumb toward his desktop.

"We have lots of money," Miles said, and John didn't correct him to say that he was the one with the money. He'd only allocated a set amount for this new start-up, and as for his personal finances, a lot of Miles's "suggestions"—like the parties and the Lamborghini—were eating into his savings.

"We need to have some income to show investors," he said, and Miles reluctantly nodded.

"I'll have updates for you by the end of the week," he said, then turned and left the office without waiting for John's reply.

When John was sure that Miles was gone, he did a quick check to make sure there wasn't anything like a key logger or other malware in place. He hated doing it, hated not trusting the only family he had left, but he couldn't take a chance.

This software was too important and too dangerous to fall into the wrong hands.

CAROLINA WOULDN'T BE back for another day, so Mia decided to go into the South Beach Security offices the next morning and finish unpacking Trey's boxes. They should have been able to do it the day before. There had only been three boxes, but somehow, they'd started chatting about all the changes that had happened in the last few months. They'd barely gotten through one box when their father had come in to haul away Trey for a meeting and then her brother had left for lunch with a client.

Having no desire to be alone, she'd left to run some errands, visit with her mother and then attend the opening of a brand-new club on Ocean Drive. But that sense of restlessness for more had lingered all day and night. She'd woken with it and, feeling like she had to do something, she'd gone back to the SBS offices to finish what she'd started the day before.

Trey was clearly surprised to see her as he walked into his office, carrying a paper bag that matched the one she'd brought with her. "I'm sorry. I should have let you know I planned on coming in."

"It's okay. I just wanted to grab a bite before…a client came in," he said and placed his bag beside hers on the table.

"I can go if you want," she said and gestured to his door, sensing he was uneasy about the upcoming meeting.

He stopped her with a raised hand. "No need. I have some time before the meeting," he said as he sat down at the table and took out his *café con leche* and toast.

She joined him and did the same, removing the contents from both bags. "Anyone interesting?" she asked.

Her brother hesitated, surprising her. Seeing his discomfort, she said, "I understand, Trey. I get that the company has to keep some things confidential."

"You know I would share if I could," Trey said and held the coffee cup between his hands as if warming them.

"I understand, but if you need my help with anything—"

"I know I can count on you," Trey said and took a sip of his coffee.

"I can leave once we're done or finish unpacking. Whatever you want," she said and nervously tore off a small piece of her toast to dunk in her coffee.

"We're meeting in the conference room, so feel free to stay, and thank you. I've hated staring at those boxes for the last couple of weeks," he said, finishing his cup of coffee. Then he reached for the one she'd brought, along with the toast.

Feeling even more restless than she had the day before, she said, "I've been thinking that maybe I could do more around here. Help out with things."

Trey lifted an eyebrow in surprise. "Really? What about Carolina?" he asked, clearly shocked that it seemed like she intended to break up the Twins.

With a little shrug, she said, "She knows I want to do something different, but that doesn't mean we can't continue to do a lot together."

Trey nodded in understanding. He tapped his chest on a spot over his heart. "You'll know in here when it's time for that change."

She suspected that more than anyone, Trey would know. *Change* had been his middle name lately.

"You'll be the first to know," she said with a smile and squeezed his hand.

Trey's office phone rang and he answered. "Please put Mr. Smith in the conference room and let my father, Sophie and Robbie know as well."

When he returned the receiver to the cradle, he pushed to his feet. "Duty calls."

"Mr. Smith? Not very original. What's next? Jones?" she teased.

With a grin, he jabbed a finger in the direction of the boxes. "If you're serious, once you finish that, I have other work for you to do."

Mia bobbled her head from side to side, considering his offer, and finally said, "I think I'm serious."

JOHN PULLED THE ball cap low and hunched down into the collar of his jacket, hoping to avoid being recognized by anyone in the office. He'd been careful coming over as well, walking quickly and keeping his head on a swivel to make sure no one was following him.

After Trey strolled into the conference room, he walked to some switches by the door and hit a few buttons, and the glass wall on the reception side of the room went opaque. He gestured to the wall of exterior windows and said, "Those have a privacy film. No one can see in."

"Thanks," he said and ripped off the ball cap and denim jacket, since he'd been sweltering in it with the heat and humidity of a Miami morning.

A second later, Trey's father and tech-guru cousins walked in. His father was in a bespoke suit while Trey and his cousins were casually dressed.

"I think you know everyone," Trey said.

John nodded. "I do. Mr. Gonzalez. Sophie. Robbie. Thank you so much for any help you can provide."

"Trey has told us that you're worried that someone is trying to steal the new software that you're developing," his father, Ramon, said.

"I am," John replied and opened his knapsack to remove his laptop. He set it on the table, intending to demo it, but Trey motioned for him to wait.

"Before you tell us about it, I just want to fill you in on what we've done so far," Trey said.

John nodded and sat down at the table, eager to hear, and Trey continued.

"As I mentioned yesterday during our lunch, I reached out to Equinox to discuss with them what security they had in place at your temporary office and the location for your supercomputer. I had them increase how often the guards did rounds, and I also asked them to install a few more CCTV cameras on the interior of the building with your supercomputer. Finally, I verified that they were using a top-notch alarm system on all the entrances to the supercomputer location, so we're set that way."

"That all seems good," John said, but Trey looked toward his dad, obviously still concerned.

"We have another suggestion to make, if you're willing to listen," Ramon said.

"I am. It's important to safeguard this software," John confirmed.

Trey nodded. "Good. Where security is a little lacking is at your temporary office space. They don't have 24/7 guards in the lobby and other areas and you're using the internet the building provided."

"I'm waiting for a dedicated line to be dropped for our internet access," John explained. Because his venture was so new and there were delays with installing the line, he'd had no choice but to use the building's cable to be able to work.

Trey nodded. "We have a dedicated line into this building and better security. The floor below this one is empty if you want to use it. No charge."

"That's very generous of you," John said, wondering at that kindness.

Trey must have seen his reticence. "You're a friend and you helped us in the past without hesitation."

"Okay. I appreciate that. I can make arrangements to move in whenever that's good for you," John said, thinking it wouldn't be that difficult since he only had about half a dozen employees in his new start-up.

"Great. We'll make arrangements to activate the connections on that floor and you can work with Sophie and Robbie to make sure you're happy with that and with the security we use on our network," his father said.

"I guess it's time for me to explain what I'm working on," John said.

"We'd love to hear," Sophie said, and Robbie nodded excitedly.

With a quick dip of his head, he began. "It's a new kind of AI predictive software that uses a neural network—"

"What is that exactly? In layman's terms, please," Trey asked, raising his hands to ask him to slow down and explain.

"It's a series of algorithms that mimic the actions of the human brain. You feed data into the network, and it processes it the way a human brain would," Sophia said, trying to simplify the concept for her cousin.

John nodded. "Exactly. But here's where my network might be a little different—normally a user collects and feeds in the data."

"Garbage in, garbage out," Robbie offered.

"Very true. Feed in inaccurate data and the result is suspect. Plus, it may not be all the data you need to make a truly accurate prediction," John said and continued with his explanation.

"I've created this kind of digital vacuum that can suck in data from dozens of sources. Social-media accounts. News articles. Credit reports. User-provided data. You name it. It's probably 10 times, if not 100 times, the amount of data that a user typically feeds into a program to prepare a report," he said, popped open his laptop and Sophie handed him a piece of paper with SBS's network password.

He logged in using a VPN for security reasons and pulled up a very rudimentary dashboard. "Sorry if this looks a little wonky, but I'm still working on the front end and some of the reporting features."

"Can you show us how it works? Predict something," Trey asked.

"What do you want to know?" John asked because Trey's question had been so open-ended.

With a boyish grin, he said, "How long will Roni and I be married?"

"Forever, hopefully," Sophie said with an eye roll, obviously exasperated.

John typed in Trey's real name—Ramon Gonzalez III—and ran the program. "This may take several minutes."

"Minutes? To process that much data? How fast is your supercomputer?" Sophie asked.

With a shrug, John said, "Not as speedy as Summit at the Oak Ridge National Laboratory, but I'm hoping to expand it and do some optimization to make it faster."

"Wow, that's fast," Robbie said with a low whistle.

"Aren't you worried about garbage in from all these different sources?" Ramon said while they waited for the program to spit out a result.

"It is possible you'll get some junk, especially if you're dealing with someone who normally generates a lot of trash news stories, like some celebrities," John clarified.

"What do you do in a situation like that?" Trey asked.

John didn't get a chance to answer because his computer dinged to let him know he had a preliminary report, but as he looked at it, he felt the blood drain from his face and a chill fill his core.

"Something wrong?" Trey asked, his sharp blue gaze picking up on John's discomfort.

"Something wonky. Let me tweak something here," he said. He looked at the code to confirm all was in order and then commanded the program to run the analysis once more.

"I'm just going to do it again. It may still be glitchy," he said, not wanting to believe the result the program was providing.

He sat there staring at the screen but didn't fail to miss how the family members gathered around the table were leaning forward, anxiously awaiting the result.

When it came, it wasn't very different, and he slumped back in his chair, his body feeling almost boneless.

"John. What is it?" Trey pressed.

With a shaky hand, John pointed in the direction of the monitor on the far wall. "Can I cast to that?"

Sophie nodded and picked up a remote. After pushing a few buttons, she said, "It's ready."

He did and a collective gasp went up around the room at the risk-assessment table.

"This report says we'll be married less than a month? It's got to be wrong," Trey said, shifting his head vehemently back and forth in denial.

"It's worse than that, Trey," Sophie said, and at his questioning look, she added, "It says you'll be dead in a month."

Chapter Three

Mia was walking past the conference room when she heard the ruckus going on inside. It was loud enough to draw the attention of the SBS employees with cubicles close to the room. They were poking their heads above the panels like meerkats coming out of their dens. The receptionist at the nearby front desk was trying to act as if she hadn't noticed something was up.

Since the privacy glass had been engaged—meaning they didn't want any attention being drawn to the conference—she knocked on the door to let Trey know they were achieving the exact opposite with their noise.

Her brother jerked open the door violently and almost jumped back when he saw Mia there. "What is it, *hermanita*?"

She looked back over her shoulder to draw his gaze to the people who were now mightily trying to appear as if they hadn't been interested in whatever was going on in the conference room.

Trey looked toward their employees, and she rose on tiptoes and whispered in his ear, "You were a little loud."

Her brother grasped her arm, gently tugged her into the conference room and closed the door. "I'm sorry. We've just had a nasty surprise," he explained.

As she looked around the room, she was stunned to see John Wilson sitting there. The mysterious guest. Given the media interest in anything he did, visiting South Beach Security was bound to cause unwanted rumors and possible damage to his new start-up.

"People were noticing with all the noise," she said and jerked a thumb in the direction of the door.

"Like I said, a nasty surprise, and John was just trying to explain it," Trey said.

John started tapping away on his keyboard and while he did, he muttered, "Just taking a look at some of the data."

Mia shot her brother a questioning look and he said, "John's new software just predicted that I'll be dead in a month."

She jumped, startled, and said, "That's crazy."

"It is, but the prediction is based on existing data and that includes all that's happened in Trey's life so far. His military service. Work as a cop. The data from those roles will weigh heavily in any calculation, but now Trey's life is different, which hopefully means a different outcome," John said, nodding his head as he worked as if he was trying to convince himself of the inaccuracy of his program's prediction.

"Prove it," Mia said.

John whipped his head in her direction. "Prove it?"

She nodded. "Yes. Make a prediction about someone else. Our dad. Me. Soph. Rob. Yourself."

He stared at her hard, his hazel eyes probing as he assessed her suggestion. With a nod, he said, "Makes sense. But not your dad. His background is too similar to Trey's."

"Your software isn't 100 percent accurate?" she said, crossing her arms and cocking a hip in challenge.

A flush of hot color swept across his cheeks and guilt slammed into her. She liked John and she hadn't meant to cut him down at the knees, but she also didn't like his software's stupid prediction about Trey.

"It's been right on everything else so far," he defended.

"Like what?" Sophie asked and stepped around to watch John as he worked.

"FOOTBALL GAMES. STOCKS. Various local elections," John said, and Sophie handed him a piece of paper with everyone's full names and dates of birth. Glancing down at the paper, he typed in Sophie's info. He sat back in the chair, his heart pounding as he waited for the results, but the program predicted the same outcome for Sophie.

"That makes no sense," he muttered and then quickly returned to the keyboard to enter Robbie's data.

Unlike the earlier noise in the room, it was deathly silent as the program ran its routine, but the prediction remained the same.

"There's got to be a bug," Sophie said, but John shook his head defiantly.

"There isn't. I've tried it over and over, including some older celebrities, and it worked," John said.

"How? Where does it get the information for life longevity?" Robbie asked and came over to stand behind him and next to Sophie.

"It accesses various actuarial tables. I even did it for myself," John explained, which prompted a chorus of questions.

"What did it say?" Sophie asked.

"How old?" Robbie said.

"When did you do it?" Trey asked.

"A ripe old age and I did it several weeks ago," John answered while his mind raced for explanations as to why his program had suddenly gone awry.

"Try it again," Mia prompted, and he peered up at her. Her blue-eyed gaze was dark and intense, and she still stood there in that defiant stance. He understood. His program had just decided to decimate her family without any apparent reason.

"I will," he said, certain of what the program would say. But if it did, he worried what that meant for the various Gonzalez family members.

He plugged in his details and waited, fingers drumming on the table. When the program spit out the answer, he sucked in a surprised breath.

"Doesn't look like a ripe old age to me," Robbie said glibly, earning a sharp elbow from his sister, Sophie.

"It's got to be a glitch," John said and opened up the source code, uncaring of the fact that Robbie and Sophie stood behind him, because if the coding wasn't wrong…

"Maybe it isn't a glitch. What's the one thing that's changed in your life since you did it?" Mia said as she relaxed her stance and began pacing back and forth by the table.

He wanted to say "Her." Nothing in his life had been the same since the day they'd first gone out together and since he'd become involved with the various members of South Beach Security. That was the connection.

"SBS," he said, which made Mia whirl to face him.

"SBS? Could that really be the connection?" she said and walked back to his side to write down her information on the piece of paper. She also added the details for

Trey's fiancée, Roni, whom John understood was one of Mia's best friends.

He plugged in Roni's name first and waited, his body stiff to match the tension radiating from the trio who now stood behind him, watching. When it came, the answer was not unexpected.

He repeated the analysis with Mia only to arrive at the same conclusion several long minutes later.

Something else occurred to him then. Something possibly more sinister than the connection to South Beach Security. "We need benchmarks. Someone who isn't a family member who works for SBS and a Gonzalez family member who doesn't work with you," John said, his mind whirling as he ran through other possible permutations if these didn't work.

"Pepe never works with us," Ramon said and wrote out his nephew's information on a piece of paper he handed to John.

Trey held up a finger, picked up the phone and dialed out. "Julia. Would you mind sharing your full name and birth date?" He jotted down the info their receptionist supplied and handed the slip of paper to him.

"Here goes nothing," John said as he entered the receptionist's information.

The Gonzalez family members had drifted away to quietly chat among themselves, and John understood. But even though he did, their actions made him feel the way he had so much of his life: like an outsider.

But then Mia hurried over, laid a hand on his shoulder and gave a reassuring squeeze. He glanced up at her and her blue-eyed gaze was understanding, but worried. Despite that, she said, "Whatever it is, we will handle this."

He didn't know if the *we* included him. He wanted it to. He wanted that and more, especially with Mia, but she had rabbited after their last time alone, needing space, she said.

"We will," he said, but it sounded almost robotic, and she clearly picked up on that and more.

"It is a *we*, John. We will do this together," Mia stressed.

He nodded and reluctantly pulled his gaze from hers back to the screen. This time the response was quite different, luckily for the receptionist. But that also raised a very scary possibility: that this was directly related to the Gonzalez family working with SBS.

His fingers felt as heavy as an anchor as he typed in the information for Pepe Gonzalez. Mia stayed by his side, her hand on his shoulder, the weight of it comforting. Welcome, especially as she swept it across his back, soothing him even though he imagined she was feeling her own kind of torment wondering if his program was right.

Every breath he took was measured as he tried to control the turmoil making his gut clench. As the seconds flew by, he closed his eyes, waiting for the telltale ding that warned of a prediction.

The slight tightening of her hand coincided with the damning ding.

"He's fine. Pepe is fine," Mia said with delight, which was short-lived. "What does that mean?" she asked, although he suspected she knew.

Peering around the family members gathered in the conference room, he felt as if he was the executioner on judgment day, but he had no doubt about what his program results now meant for them and for him.

"We're all in danger. Someone is going to end our lives unless we can figure it out."

MIA'S STOMACH WAS in knots as the team sat down at the table to consider John's ominous warning.

It just didn't make any sense to her as John ran the names of the other Gonzalez family members who were involved with SBS and got the same dire results. Luckily, other family members were spared.

"*Tia* Elena and *Tio* Jose are fine. So is Pepe, but not Carolina. Why is that?" Mia asked.

"Maybe because you and Caro are intimately involved with SBS even if not officially employed by it," her father said.

"What about the *abuelos*?" Trey said, worried about their grandparents, especially since *Abuelo* Ramon had been the founder of the business.

John ran them through the program but shook his head at the response. "They're fine, only... I was, too, a few weeks ago."

"Meaning?" Trey asked, a dark eyebrow raised in challenge.

"Meaning that if we fail to stop this current danger, their outcomes could change. They're only safe if we're safe," John said.

Trey muttered a curse and raked his fingers through his hair. Mia understood his frustration. Family was a priority in their lives, and they would all do whatever it took to keep their family safe.

Her brother paced back and forth while the rest of them sat around, lost in their own thoughts, until Trey whirled and said, "The last investigation with Ricky and Mariela. I thought there was something off about the attacks on them."

Mia had only been tangentially involved in that case and needed clarification. "Care to explain?"

Trey nodded, walked to the table and gripped the top of the leather executive chair. "There was a drive-by at Ricky's house that didn't connect for me because whoever had attacked Mariela the night before couldn't have possibly known to go there."

"There was a drive-by at the Del Sol when you and Roni were investigating your partner's murder," Mia pointed out.

"But drive-bys are a common gang tactic," Sophie said, adding to the discussion.

"You're right, Soph. When gang members do that, they have a specific target in mind," Trey explained.

"But they could have been targeting Mariela even if it was at Ricky's. I mean, it doesn't seem like gang members care very much about collateral damage," Mia said, sadly familiar with it since there had been quite a few of them in Miami over the years.

"What if Mariela wasn't the target? And what if whoever shot at Roni and me wasn't a member of that human-trafficking ring?" Trey mused.

Sophie glanced over at John and said, "Could your program tell us the probability that those two drive-bys were related?"

"I'd have to make a few changes to feed in just data from those two events, but, yes, it could," he said and immediately got to work on it.

Trey looked at his watch and clapped his hands. "Hard to believe, but it's almost lunch and I think we need a break so we can have fresh eyes on anything John pulls up. I'm going to have Julia order some lunch."

"Tux, tux, tux," Mia teased, ignoring that if John's predictions came true, they wouldn't be dressing for a wedding in a few months. Just funerals.

Trey ignored her jibe, picked up the phone and asked Julia, the receptionist, to order sandwiches from a nearby Jewish deli. "Tired of Cubanos," he said in response to the look she shot him.

"I never get tired of Cubanos," John muttered, fully aware of what was happening around them despite his intense attention to his laptop.

"Is there anything we can do to help?" Robbie asked as both he and Sophie sat there, itching to hit the keys on their laptops.

"Not right now, but maybe in the future," he said, and Mia was grateful that he was willing to trust them with his code. Which made her wonder... "Why did you come see us this morning?"

He shot her a brief intense look and said, "Someone's trying to steal the program."

"Is there any chance that the same person is responsible for our less-than happily-ever-afters?" Mia asked.

With a shrug, John said, "We can run that through the program as well."

By the time the deli sandwiches had arrived, John had the program pull in the data for the drive-bys from various news accounts and the reports the police had provided to SBS. While they waited for an answer, they snagged food from the platter loaded with assorted sandwiches with brisket, corned beef and pastrami, along with side dishes of coleslaw, various salads, and several types of pickles.

Mia grabbed a brisket sandwich and layered some coleslaw on it. With a laugh, John said, "A brisket po'boy."

Mia chuckled and smiled. "I guess you could call it that, especially if you're from N'awlin," she teased, mimicking what a native would call that city and hoping she might be able to learn more about him.

"Not from New Orleans," John advised and grabbed a pastrami sandwich and a sour pickle.

On their few dates, if they could be called that, he'd never really said where he was from and his bio had omitted that info, probably deliberately. Plus, he had no discernable accent to give it away. "Flyover country?" she asked because of the lack of accent.

"Nope," he said and bit into his sandwich.

Scrutinizing him, he had the kind of preppy looks that she could picture in an Ivy League school, but his bio had said nothing about that either. "New England?" she asked.

That noncommittal "Nope" came again, challenging her to try again.

There was nothing surfer-dude about him, so she eliminated California, but before she could ask, the program warned it had an answer.

John cast the answer onto the large screen for all to see. "75-percent probability the two attacks are related."

"I knew it," Trey said. "My gut told me something was off about that drive-by."

"I'm sorry we all dismissed your gut. What else did you think was off?" Sophie asked and put down her sandwich, seemingly ready to start gathering information for their next prediction.

"Mariela's husband supposedly committed suicide,

but I wasn't buying it. It just tied everything up too neatly when it was anything but neat," Trey said.

"What else?" Robbie challenged, also eager to tackle the problem.

Trey tapped his palm with his index finger, delineating the various points he was making. "If those two drive-bys were connected and had nothing to do with Mariela's ex—"

"Did whoever was behind them have something to do with her ex's death?" Sophie interrupted, connecting the dots he had laid out.

"And what does it have to do with the family and with whoever is trying to steal John's program?" Robbie said.

"John? What do you think?" Mia asked, since he'd remained silent during the discussion.

He sucked in a deep breath, held it for a long moment and roughly blew it out. "I think we need as much data as we can get about all those events and you two—" he pointed at Sophie and Robbie "—need access to the program."

That statement sent Trey, her cousins and John into a flurry of action, leaving her father and her waiting for them to work their magic.

Her father's face was set in a deep glower, full of worry and anger. She walked over and laid a hand on his arm, much as she'd seen her mother do so often when he'd come home bothered about something at work. As her mother had done more than once, she said, "I know you're worried, but we'll figure it out."

His rough grunt wasn't reassuring, so she tried again. "What are you worrying about, *Papi*?"

"Everything," he said and shook his head. "It's all too much to believe. Predictions. Software."

"But it's real, *Papi*. AI can even help doctors diagnose schizophrenia," she said, recalling a recent article she had seen when she had been trying to understand what it was that John did to earn his millions.

Her father harrumphed and pointed first to his head, then to his heart and finally to a midsection that was still surprisingly flat for a sixtysomething. "Trey's gut said something was wrong weeks ago. I should have listened."

"*We* should have listened, *Papi*," she said, wanting to lift some of the weight he carried off his shoulders. It was one of the reasons she'd been happy that Trey had decided to join SBS. It was time to share that burden and pass it on to someone younger to handle.

It also reminded her of the discussion she'd had with her brother earlier. It wasn't fair for Trey to have to shoulder that burden alone and hopefully she could help him.

"Sit down and have something to eat. Let them do whatever and then we can decide how to proceed," she said, hoping to ease his worries.

"*Gracias, mi'ja,*" he said and offered her the flicker of a smile, confirming that she had successfully channeled her mother to tame the bear.

She walked back to grab her sandwich and soda, and moved to her father's side, offering him her support while they waited for the others to work their magic. They had finished their sandwiches and brought in coffee when Sophie got the first ding from the program.

As John had done before, she displayed her result on

the large screen. "70-percent probability that Mariela's husband didn't commit suicide."

"I don't need to have a program to tell me that whoever attacked Ricky and Mariela is responsible," Trey said, and from beside her, his father grunted his agreement.

Barely a minute later, a second ding burst from Robbie's computer with an answer, and he immediately popped the image onto the screen. "Whoever killed her ex…the probability is 85 percent that they'll be responsible for our deaths."

"So we solve her ex's murder—" Trey began.

"We stop our own," Mia said, finishing for him.

Another ding sounded from John's laptop, but he muttered a curse when he saw the answer.

"What's the matter?" Mia asked.

John shook his head and finally displayed the response. "Only 50-percent probability that it's the same person who's trying to steal the software."

"That's okay, John," Trey said. "It just means we have two cases to investigate. Are you all ready? Mia?"

She knew why he had singled her out. It wasn't just their earlier conversation to work more at SBS, it was because John was involved. But just because she had her doubts about any kind of relationship with the tech millionaire, even a friendly one, when family was involved, there was only one answer she could give.

"I'm ready."

Chapter Four

He had to get this right because he wasn't sure they'd have another chance to do it, he thought.

John Wilson hadn't noticed the tracking software loaded on his phone.

He was barely two blocks away and on the move. That meant he'd be in the office in no time.

Great.

He sent out a short text to warn his hired muscle that he had to be ready to move.

Looking at the phone again, he held his breath, counting down until he saw the blip on the phone turn toward their building.

It wouldn't take more than a few minutes for John to take the elevator to the floor. He texted his accomplice to tell him to get on the move.

Sucking in a deep breath, he prepped himself for the attack.

John was surprised when Mia slipped her arm through his as they took the short walk to his temporary office space.

"Try not to look so grumpy," Mia said and faked a bright laugh, as if he'd said something funny.

John forced a smile he wasn't feeling and leaned his head close to hers. They'd shown up in some tabloids and gossip sites when they'd first been spotted together, so it made perfect sense to fake it in case someone was following them.

"Better?" he said, and this time Mia laughed for real.

"Seriously, John. You look like the crazed clown in those *It* movies," she said and playfully tugged on his arm to urge him to loosen up.

"Pennywise?"

She furrowed her brow, obviously confused. "Pennywise? I didn't know that was his name."

"That is the crazy clown's name. I guess you're not into horror movies," he said and shot a quick glance at her.

She wrinkled her nose and shook her head. "Too scary for me."

He had to remember that because it was too tempting to picture her curled beside him, watching a movie. But not a scary one. Maybe one of his black-and-white classics.

"I'll keep that in mind," he said, but she immediately shut him down.

"Just going to your office to help you assess what it'll take to move," she said, but with a smile, in case anyone was watching.

"A shame. I have a really nice entertainment system at my house," he said.

"We never went to your house. Why is that?" she asked, that furrow on her brow marring her flawless skin again.

He paused to look at her and smooth a finger across the crease. "Do you really want to know?"

She nodded and he dipped his hand down to swipe his thumb across her cheek. "I'm a very private person."

She smirked and arched her perfectly manicured eyebrows. "Really? The Del Sol parties. The Lamborghini? They don't scream *private* to me."

He blew out a harsh breath and shook his head before resuming the walk to his temporary office space. "Those are all Miles's doing. He thinks I need a certain image."

"Really? Like, 'I need to show I have a bigger—'"

"Yes, like that. I'm not a fan of it, but he's my brother," John admitted as they walked into the building, and he badged them through the security checkpoint.

"Isn't he your half brother?" she asked, and he shrugged.

"He's my only family, so as far as I'm concerned, he's my brother," he said and her gaze grew dark, almost troubled.

"I guess that's something else you want to keep private. You don't say much about your family," she said and shot him a quick look from the corner of her eye.

With another, heavier shrug and a frown, he said, "Not much to tell. We're not like your family."

To her credit, she left it at that, sensing it was a topic that not only troubled him, but also probably caused him pain.

As soon as they walked into their temporary offices, the young woman who was manning the reception desk smiled at them. "Good afternoon, John."

"Good afternoon, Rachel. Could you please send an email blast to everyone—"

The loud bang of a door slamming against a wall jerked his attention to the end of the hall.

A masked man rushed out of the stairway entrance and raced toward them, gun drawn.

John shoved Mia behind him and shouted at Rachel. "Call 911."

John braced for the attack, but barely a breath later, Miles rushed out of his office and threw himself at the masked man.

Muttering a curse under his breath, John rushed forward to help his brother, who was grappling with the intruder. But a second later the man pistol-whipped Miles, threw him off and scrambled to his feet. The man backtracked toward the stairway, seemingly surprised that it hadn't gone as planned, and then sped away, passing by several of their workers, who were standing at their office doors, immobilized by shock.

John reached Miles, who had sat up and was leaning against the wall, dazed. A thin trickle of blood ran down the side of his face from a cut on his brow.

Mia was there a second later as John kneeled by his brother. "Are you okay?" he asked.

Miles shook his head as if trying to clear away the shock of the attack. He reached up, his hand shaky, touched his brow and winced. When Miles pulled back his fingers and saw the blood, his face paled.

John laid a hand on his shoulder as Mia handed him a small handkerchief to staunch the blood. John gently placed it on Miles's brow, but his brother winced again.

"Sorry." John looked up at Mia and said, "Could you ask Rachel to call for an ambulance?"

Miles waved his hand. "No. I'm okay. Just a little shaken."

"Can you stand up?" Mia asked.

Miles did a wobbly nod and when John offered his hand, he grasped it and unsteadily got to his feet.

"Let's get you cleaned up," Mia said just as a pair of security guards rushed through the front doors, followed by two Miami police officers.

John glanced toward the door. "Can you help Miles while I talk to the police?"

Mia nodded. "I can."

MIA WATCHED AS John went to speak to the authorities, and after, helped Miles back into his office, where he sat on the couch. Seconds later, a pale and flustered Rachel rushed in. "Here's a first-aid kit."

"Thanks. Could you please get us some water?" she said. Giving the young woman something to do would hopefully make her calm down.

"Sure. I'll be back in a second," Rachel said and rushed from the room.

"Smooth move," Miles said and smiled, but then winced, the movement obviously bringing him pain.

As much as she disliked Miles, she respected what he had done to protect his brother. "That was a brave move. The man was armed."

She sat on a coffee table in front of the sofa where Miles was and laid the first-aid kit at her side. She opened it, took out some alcohol pads and ripped them open.

"This might sting," she said and dabbed at the cut to wipe away the blood that had trailed down his face.

Miles grimaced and sucked in a breath, but then said, "He's my brother. I had to protect him."

She didn't correct him the way she had John before. She sensed being more than half brothers was important to them, but she also sensed something else. Something that was troubling her, but that she couldn't really put a finger on.

"You could have been shot." She grabbed some butterfly bandages to apply to the small cut on his brow.

"I wasn't really thinking about that." He shrugged, and the movement was so much like John's, it was impossible to deny they were related by blood. But as his hazel gaze locked with hers, he rubbed her the wrong way again. His eyes might be the same color as John's but there was a deadness there that worried her.

A knock on the door drew her attention to John and two police officers, one female and one male, standing there.

"The police have some questions for you, Miles. You, too, Mia," John said, his handsome face all hard lines.

She nodded, not that she had much info to provide. But she sat there patiently as the police questioned Miles, jotting down anything he remembered. But as he had before, something struck her as off about his testimony. Almost as if it was too pat. Rehearsed, which was impossible considering how quickly the situation had all gone down.

"Miss Gonzalez?" one officer said. She was a twentysomething that Mia had seen patrolling the area more than once when she'd visited her family's agency.

"I'm sorry. Did you ask me something?" She'd been too focused on Miles and hadn't heard the young woman's question.

"What can you tell us about what happened?" the officer asked.

Mia took a moment to mentally run through the incident. With a nod, she said, "A masked man raced out of the stairway access. He must have come in through a service area to avoid lobby security. There's hopefully CCTV footage from that area."

She jotted down the info and said, "Thank you. Anything else?"

Mia nodded. "He was hunched a little as he ran at us, but based on the height of the doorframe, I would say he was at least six feet tall, maybe a little more. A little heavier than medium build. Right-handed. He held the gun in his right hand. I think it was a 9mm Glock and he was either white or white Hispanic."

As the male officer narrowed his gaze as if in challenge, Mia circled her index finger around her eyes. "The mask exposed the area around his eyes. Brown, I think."

His gaze narrowed even more and in an accusatory tone the officer said, "You seem to have seen a lot in a really short time."

The female police officer elbowed him. "That's Detective Gonzalez's sister," she said and that seemed to explain everything to the other officer.

"Sorry. I didn't mean to offend," he said.

"That's okay, Officer Johnson. I guess I've hung out with my brother too much."

"We know him well. He was a great detective and is missed on the force," the female said.

"Thank you, Officer Puente. I'll let him know," she said with a slow dip of her head.

"I think we have all we need, but we'd recommend you going to the hospital to get that checked out. It looks like he hit you pretty hard," Officer Puente said and gestured to the makeshift bandage Mia had applied to Miles's brow.

"I agree," John said and looked at her.

"Why don't you take your brother to the hospital? I'll take care of things here," she said.

"I'd appreciate that, Mia. Thank you," he said, then helped Miles to his feet and walked out with him, followed by the police officers.

Mia waited until they were gone before dialing Trey. When he answered, she said, "We have a problem."

JOHN PACED BACK and forth in the waiting area for the emergency room, anxious for any word from the doctor on his brother's condition. The knapsack containing his laptop dragged at his shoulder, but since it was the only machine that could access the full code for his program, he took it with him everywhere unless he locked it up at home.

In his mind's eye, he ran through what had happened and what else he could have done during the attack. His first concerns had been for Mia and Rachel until Miles had rushed out of the office and engaged the intruder.

That was when he'd sprang into action, but by the time he'd gotten there, Miles had already been hurt and the intruder had been on the run.

Clearly, the masked man hadn't had a taste for more violence, but if that was the case, why break into a crowded office at midday, armed and masked?

As someone who was supposedly a genius and a problem solver, it bothered him that he couldn't wrap his head around the motivation behind what had happened. That made him feel even more useless considering how little info he'd been able to provide the police.

Not like Mia. He had been impressed with all the observations she made in the space of scant seconds.

Hopefully enough for the police to move their investigation along.

A doctor in a standard white jacket approached him. "Mr. Wilson?"

John glanced at the man's nametag. "Dr. Castillo. Thank you for taking care of my brother. How is he?"

The doctor motioned to his brow. "Small cut that someone very capably butterflied. No signs of a concussion, but sometimes it takes hours for symptoms to show up."

"Nothing's broken, right?" John said and peered toward the ER, where he could see his brother resting on a bed.

"Nothing broken from what I can see, but I think we should take Miles down for some X-rays to confirm and I'd like to keep him overnight to watch for those concussion symptoms. You can see him now before we send him for the X-rays," the doctor said and pointed the chart at Miles.

"Thanks, I will," John said and hurried in to see his brother.

Miles's eyes were closed, but as John laid a hand on his arm, he opened them, almost sleepily, making John worry that he might have a concussion.

"How are you feeling?" John said.

"Tired. Sleepy."

"Doctor doesn't think there are any internal injuries but they're going to do X-rays to confirm and keep you overnight in case you have a concussion," John explained.

Miles nodded and offered him a weak smile. "I'll be okay."

"That was a stupid thing to do," John said and squeezed Miles's arm.

"He was heading for you. I had to do something. Mom always said I had to protect you," Miles said, rousing memories of the two of them huddled in a closet, hiding from John's dad as he beat on their mom.

"I know and I can't thank you enough." John knew his brother wouldn't appreciate what he was about to tell him.

"I'm moving our offices to a more secure location."

Miles jerked back, clearly surprised. "Is that really necessary?"

"I think it is," he said and watched the slow rise of color creep up his brother's neck.

"And I guess what you say goes," Miles said. For as long as John could remember, Miles had hated John being the one calling the shots, especially since Miles was the older brother and presumably the one who should be in charge.

"I appreciate all that you've done for me, but when it comes to the company—"

"It's your baby. I get it," he bit out, his anger impossible to miss.

"Let's not fight, Miles. All I care about right now is knowing that you're okay." John squeezed his brother's arm again in reassurance.

With a few abrupt nods, Miles said, "Sure. I'm fine. You go take care of things. I'll be okay."

"I'll see you later. Try and get some rest," John said, rose and bro-hugged him before walking out the door.

As he exited the emergency room and flagged down a cab, he dialed Mia.

"How is it going?" he asked.

"People have packed their personal items and computers. Trey has a truck waiting for us in the delivery area. We'll be waiting for you at the SBS building so you can direct people on where to go," Mia advised.

"I'll be there in about a half hour. Thank you for taking care of things," he said.

"Of course. I hope Miles is okay," she said, and in the background, he could hear the hushed murmur of people talking.

"He is. I'll go back later to check in on him. See you soon," he said, then leaned forward and provided the address to the cabbie, who had been patiently waiting for him to end the call.

The cabbie whipped out of the emergency-room area and headed for the highway to take them to downtown Miami.

John bounced his legs up and down, anxious to get to the building so they could finish the move and get settled. He was sure his people would need an explanation for what was happening, and he needed to figure out what were the necessary next steps they had to take to find out who was behind the attacks on his servers and on Miles.

Miles, he thought, recalling his fear as the gunman had rushed in and his brother had challenged him.

But what could the gunman have expected to do? Kidnap me? he wondered.

If they had him, they could force him to give up the code, and then what? Was his code worth such a risk? he asked himself, but the answer was clear.

Yes.

He had no doubt that if the code got into the wrong hands, it could be used for all the wrong reasons. Stock manipulations that could take down companies and exchanges, destroying people's livelihoods and national economies. Warfare games that would lead to real-life conflicts and deaths.

John's mind whirled with the many ways lives could be changed by the misuse of his code, and more than likely not for the better, like the predictions that his software had made for himself and the various Gonzalez family members.

Dead in a month.

It boggled his mind, which was why he had to get to his people and the Gonzalez family and work on stopping the threat to the family and to his software.

As the cab pulled up in front of the building, he threw open the door, tapped his card to pay for the ride and handed the driver a generous tip in cash. "Thank you," he said and met the driver's eyes in the rearview mirror.

The driver offered him a sympathetic nod, obviously aware that all was not well, since he'd picked up John at the hospital.

With an abrupt nod in response, John rushed toward the doors of the SBS building, but as he hurried inside, it occurred to him that he didn't have a badge to clear security. But when he looked toward the desk with the security guards, Mia stepped out of an elevator and walked toward the guards.

Although *walk* was a tame way to describe the way she moved. Confident. Sexy as hell in those impossibly high heels that made her long legs look even longer. She was focused on her phone, but when she looked up and saw him, she smiled.

That smile did all kinds of things to his insides. Joy. Something he'd rarely experienced in his early life.

Need. And not just sexual need. It was a soul-deep need from a man who was tired of being alone. Tired of being seen as something he wasn't.

That smile stayed on her face while her eyes darkened and narrowed, as if reaching inside him and finding that need.

"You okay?" she asked as she walked up to him and tenderly laid her hand on his arm.

That touch, so freely given and full of concern, gentled the turmoil in his soul.

I am now, he thought but didn't say, afraid to reveal too much to her given their unsettled relationship.

"Thank you for everything," he said, which made her purse her lips with annoyance as she realized he was shutting her out.

With a nod, she reached into the pocket of her jacket and handed him a building badge.

"I hope you don't mind that we took some liberties for your photo," she said.

He examined the picture and realized it was a cropped version of a selfie that Mia had taken on one of their dates. It kindled memories of that date and how much fun they'd had. How happy he'd been.

"I don't mind," he said, although the photo would remind him every day of what he wanted with her and didn't have. *Yet*, he thought hopefully.

She flipped an elegant hand toward the security desk and the gold bangles at her wrist jangled musically. "The badge clears you for your new floor, the SBS floors and the penthouse suite."

He inched up an eyebrow in question. "Penthouse suite?"

She nodded and pushed the button for the elevator.

"We have a space for family and guests to use if they need to stay overnight. I can show it to you later."

"Thanks, although I'm not sure I'll need it. I have the suite at the Del Sol—"

She wrinkled her nose at the mention of that since it was clearly distasteful to her.

"I'm not a fan of it either," he said as the elevator arrived. They stepped into it and she inserted her badge.

"If you're not a fan, why do you do it?" she pressed.

With a careless shrug, he said, "Miles thinks we need to keep ourselves in the public eye."

"I guess that explains the Lamborghini, too?" she said with a quick side-glance.

He offered up another shrug. "The Lamborghini, too. It's an amazing ride, but I'd rather not call so much attention to myself."

The glance she gave him this time was longer and more thoughtful. Her voice was a touch softer as she said, "Then why don't you say no?"

"It's important to Miles and he's always been there for me. I feel like it's the least I can do."

The ding warned them they had reached their destination and they stepped out of the elevator and into a beautifully appointed space, where Rachel was already at a curved reception desk that could easily sit another person. The base of the desk was the rich color of Cuban coffee and topped with a frosted white glass counter. The wall behind the desk was covered in colored stones that enhanced the deep hues of the wood and at its base were matching storage cabinets.

"Are you doing okay?" he asked Rachel, certain the young woman might be rattled by all that had happened in the last few hours.

Rachel offered a weak smile and shake of her head. "I am. How is Miles?"

"He's fine, thank you. If you're all set up, why don't you take the rest of the day off. I'm sure you could use some time to relax," he said, but Rachel shook her head.

"I'm fine, really. But if you want, I could help you or some of the others unpack," she said.

"That would be nice. Why don't you check with the others to see if they need your help?"

The receptionist shot him a strained smile, rose and walked down the hall to assist their other employees.

Mia leaned close and whispered in his ear, "She's got a crush on you."

"Does she?" he asked and looked back over his shoulder at Rachel before she ducked into one of the other offices.

"She does. Who wouldn't?" Mia bit her lip at what she'd said and waved her hands to stop him. "I mean, a young girl like her is bound to be impressed by someone like you."

"But not a sophisticated older woman like you," he teased and loved the flush of color that swept up her neck to her face.

She ignored his comment and led him to the farthest point of the hall, where there was a space for another desk and, beyond that, an immense corner office. The door was open, but as they walked in, Mia said, "This door is also controlled by the badge in case you want to lock it."

He nodded, walked to the wall of windows and let his knapsack gently slip to the floor. Sucking in a deep breath, he almost inhaled the beautiful panorama of the parks and marinas along the waterfront, the assorted causeways and bridges leading to Miami Beach and, in the distance, Biscayne Bay and Brickell Key.

"This is really nice. Thank you," he said and faced her.

"Whenever you're ready, we're on the next floor up," she said and pointed her perfectly manicured index finger toward the ceiling. "Trey is reviewing the police reports for today's attack and Sophie and Robbie have been working on some things as well."

"Let me just give my people a heads-up and then we can go. I'll unpack later," he said, then picked up his knapsack, slung it over his shoulder, approached her and laid a hand at the small of her back to gently urge her out.

"Sure. That probably makes the most sense. This way you can visit Miles as well before it gets too late."

They walked back toward the front lobby and the reception area. Just to the left of the stone wall behind the reception desk was a large conference room. "Why don't you wait for me there?"

She nodded and he walked down the hall to where a number of employees were unpacking their areas. He rounded them up and herded them to the conference room.

When they were all seated there, he offered them a smile that he hoped would reassure them. "I know what happened today was scary. Luckily no one was seriously hurt."

"Is Miles okay?" Rachel asked, wringing her hands together.

"He is, thank you. And moving here, into this more secure area, will make sure all of you will be okay as well. But as you can imagine, it's important we keep what happened and this move confidential so as to not hurt the company," John said and was pleased to see the nods of everyone seated around the table.

"Good. I'm glad you're all on board. Since you may need a little time to deal with this change, feel free to take the rest of the day and tomorrow off."

"No need, John. At least not for me. If you don't mind, I'm going to finish unpacking and get back to work," said Oliver York, one of the programmers who had been with him since day one.

The murmured agreement of the others around the table filled John with hope and satisfaction. "Thank you, all. I truly appreciate it," he said and laid a hand over his heart in emphasis.

When his employees had drifted out of the conference room and back to their offices, Mia walked over to him.

"They are all so very loyal. That's impressive," she said and slipped her arm through his.

"I'm lucky to have them," he said. *And you*, he thought.

Together they strolled to the elevator. Once inside, Mia slipped in her badge and pressed the button for the floor above them.

In no time they were there, and as they entered, a young Latina receptionist greeted them with a warm smile. "Good afternoon, Mia. Mr. Smith," Julia said with almost a wink since she had obviously realized who he was.

"John, please, Julia," he said and smiled.

"John. Mia. Everyone is in the conference room," Julia said and motioned behind her to the room where the opaque window glass was still in place. It was clear when they entered that Trey, Sophie and Robbie had news for them.

Chapter Five

Mia hurried to the table, where Trey was hovering behind Sophie and Robbie as they worked, his large hands resting on the backs of their chairs as he leaned forward to look at their laptops.

"Looks like you found something," Mia said and ambled to a spot at the table where she had earlier left her purse.

Trey flicked a hand in the direction of the large television on the far wall of the conference room. "Why don't you put up that analysis, Sophie," he said.

With the push of the remote and a few clicks on her keyboard, Sophie cast her laptop to the television.

Mia recognized the financial summary and chart for the start-up that John had recently sold. The mountain-style chart was appropriate considering that the peak of it was as high as Everest at the time John had sold it. But even she could see that in the midst of that growth there was one big chasm where the stock's price had bottomed.

She gestured to it. "What was going on there?"

John walked up to the TV and pointed to the drop. "The press got hold of bad news about a problem we were having with one of our important programs."

"Do you know how that happened?" Trey asked and tucked his arms across his broad chest.

With a shrug, John said, "I'm not sure, but I always suspected someone leaked the news to a reporter."

"To short the stock?" Mia asked, thinking someone could have made quite a bit of money from selling the stock at its high at the time and buying it back when it bottomed out.

"And if it was someone in the company, they could face charges for insider trading," John said, lips in a tight line that communicated so much to her.

"You think what happened today was done for the same reason?" She had earlier thought that there had been something wrong about the attack and about Miles's answers to the police.

"If it hasn't already hit some online news services, I expect it might hit the local news later tonight," John said.

In response, Robbie tapped away on his keyboard. A second later he said, "There's nothing in the news so far."

Trey added, "I reached out to some friends on the force and asked them to keep it low-key. Just a random break-in and I asked them to keep your names out of it."

"Can they do that?" John asked and dragged a hand through the waves of his light brown hair, tousling it messily.

She wanted to go over and smooth it out as she had more than once when they'd been going out, but resisted the urge.

"They can for now. If someone starts pressing, they may not be able to," Trey admitted.

If someone started pressing, Mia thought, but then

something else came to her. "What if someone did the attack for another reason?"

Trey moved away from their cousins and toward the conference-room table. Leaning on a chair there, he eyeballed her. "Like to cover something up?"

With those words, John hurried back to the table and his knapsack. He yanked out his laptop and sat down in front of it. "Like if something had been stolen?" he said and started tapping away at the keys.

"Or if they wanted to hide what they were doing. Are you going to run it through your program?" Mia asked.

"I am," he said and nodded.

"Robbie and I are going to try and see what we can find out about the kinds of transactions that went on during that short-selling period," Sophie said as she got to work on her laptop.

"If it was an insider, they probably did it through a holding company to avoid filing a Section 16 report with the SEC," Mia said.

Trey chuckled and shook his head. "I always knew you were more than just a pretty face."

A beautiful face, she thought she heard John murmur under his breath, but as she glared at him, he appeared to be buried in whatever he was doing on his laptop.

"The one thing they most likely wanted to steal is your program, but from what I can see, you always take your laptop with you," Mia said and glanced toward the battle-scarred leather bag that John took virtually everywhere.

"I usually carry it with me except when I lock it up at night, but you're right. It goes everywhere because it's the only way to fully access the code," John confirmed with a bop of his head.

"But that would be a really low-tech way to steal something very high-tech," Sophie said, her brow heavily furrowed over her deep blue eyes.

"They would still have to hack your password to get in," Robbie said.

"It takes multiple passwords to log in and on top of that, they'd need to know how to piece together everything to have the full work of code. Not likely a run-of-the-mill burglar could do that," he said and closed his laptop. Barely a beat later, he added, "Based on local crime data, the nature of the crime and other variables, the program rules out that it was an actual robbery or attack."

"Which means it was planned to hide something," Trey said.

"Like who might be working for you who wants to short the stock," Mia said.

"Or who wants to steal the code. That's why you first came to us, after all," Trey added to the discussion.

"Or someone who wants to do both," Sophie said, earning an agreeing grunt from Robbie.

Trey sat down and gestured for Mia to join him, the cousins and John at the table.

Mia did, but her mind was running through all the variables of who would fake an attack and why. Miles's face immediately came to mind. She kept that thought to herself as Trey said, "If you had to short-list who might want to do this—"

John waved his hands to stop Trey. "Short-list? For real? I trust them. It's why I kept these particular people for this new venture after I sold my start-up."

Mia leaned over and laid a hand on John's as it rested

on the surface of the table. "I know this must be hard for you."

"You can't imagine. They've been with me for years, and Miles… He's my brother," he said and drove his fingers through his hair in agitation.

"It's obvious this is difficult for you so why don't we take emotion out of this," Mia said and peered at his closed laptop.

It was obvious what she wanted him to do, but he shook his head, as if in disbelief. "You want me to use the program?"

"It calculates probabilities, doesn't it? Let the program tell us who is on the short list," she said, and Trey murmured his agreement.

"She's got a point, John. The program takes any and all feelings out of the decision."

John looked between the two of them and then over to Sophie and Robbie, who nodded, almost in unison.

With a heavy sigh, John opened his laptop, but paused with his fingers over the keys. "This may take a while. There's Miles and about half a dozen employees."

"We'll wait. In the meantime, we'll get to work on some other investigations about the stock transactions and I'll reach out to the police to see if they have anything else on today's attack," Trey said.

John nodded, but his face was set in harsh lines, his lips in a knife-sharp slash. His hazel eyes had grown muddied, almost lifeless, as he entered in the information.

Needing something to do because it was distressing to see how pained he was by the possibility of one of his people being a traitor, she got up and got him paper and a pen in case he needed to jot something down. She also went out to grab some of the menus that the receptionist kept, since she suspected they'd be working right through dinner.

John had said that he wanted to go visit Miles at the hospital—maybe it would make sense to take a break before dinner and visit before it got too late.

When she went back inside, John was writing something down, while Sophie and Robbie were seated on the other side of the table, busy working. Trey had left the room through a side door, probably to call his friends at the police department.

She sat beside John again, but took a moment to swipe through her social-media accounts as well as some other sources she followed that carried local news and events.

There was no mention of what had happened earlier and beneath her breath she thanked Trey's connections for doing as they had promised.

As she swiped through her various accounts, she caught John's actions as he added names to the paper along with a number. She suspected the numbers were for the probability of their being on the short list.

The list grew longer until there was only one name left to add, but she noticed John hesitating.

She leaned close and in a soft whisper, she said, "I know you don't want to do it."

"I don't," he said and muttered a curse beneath his breath. "He's my brother."

Half, she wanted to remind him, but didn't because she understood the importance of family, especially to him since he seemed to have lacked it in his life.

"Isn't it better to rule him out instead of having doubt eat at you?" she urged.

He laid his fingers on the keys, clearly conflicted. But then he started typing away and said, "You're right. It's better to know."

As he finished and sat back to wait for the response, she held her breath and prayed for the answer that she knew he wanted.

Chapter Six

Mia had been stuck to his side like white on rice ever since the program had provided its damning accusation.

Miles had come out as Suspect #1 on their short list with a seventy-five-percent probability.

But he reminded himself of how he'd considered seventy-five a failing grade when he was in school.

So why trust that kind of number when it came to Miles? His brother. His only remaining family. Really his best friend as well, not that he had many friends, as he'd told Trey.

Trey, who held back from saying anything when John had revealed the results. He'd been almost too business-like as he'd asked John if Sophie and Robbie could run their own analysis of those on the short list.

What could I have said or done? John thought. To reject the results was to reject that his software worked, but accepting it…

"I know you're bothered," Mia said softly as she drove the Lamborghini to the hospital to see Miles.

"Wouldn't you be?" he replied, angered by the re-sults but also because in the back of his mind he'd had his doubts over the last several months. Ever since the stock had tanked, Miles had been different. That sense of Miles being off had only intensified in the last couple of months since he'd sold his start-up and begun this new venture.

"I would. Family is important to me, and I know it is to you as well," she said and, in a supportive gesture, stroked a hand down his arm.

As it had before, her touch gentled the riot of emotions that had pretzeled his gut into a painful knot.

"It is. It's just Miles and me," he admitted. He normally didn't like to talk about his personal life and had kept it from Mia in the past, but now it seemed almost useless to keep secrets. After all, if his program was right, they might be dead in a month.

"We had a tough life," he said and faltered, not sure how to continue.

"I understand," she said.

He laughed and shook his head. "You? Come on, princess. Don't play games with me. You've got a Cartier Tank watch on your wrist. If I'm not mistaken, that's a Prada bag and a Carolina Herrera dress."

"Judgy much?" she snapped, the heat of anger on her face.

"If the Louboutin fits—"

"I've earned my money but in case you care to know, things weren't always easy for my family either. Not when my grandparents came from Cuba or when my dad was a cop or in the marines. I don't know how my mom did it sometimes, but we always had food on the table and a roof over our heads," she said, her tone sharp and filled with pain.

He hadn't known that and wouldn't have guessed because of the current success of the family.

"I'm sorry," he said and pulled off the highway and onto the road leading to the hospital.

The silence in the car was as heavy as a thousand-pound boulder as he finished the drive to Jackson Memorial. They parked and walked in silence into the building. After checking in at the lobby, they hurried up to Miles's room only to find that it was empty.

"Wait here," John said and headed to the nurses' station to find out where Miles was, but as he neared the station and heard a very feminine giggle, he knew.

Miles was in a wheelchair and chatting up a twentysomething nurse who was clearly eating up the attention.

The young woman looked in his direction, which also drew Miles's gaze to him. The broad, welcoming smile that had been on his face a moment before faded slightly.

"Bro. I wasn't expecting you," Miles said.

"I promised you I'd be back," John reminded him as he walked over, then took hold of the handles of the wheelchair. As John swiveled the chair back in the direction of his room, he leaned close to Miles and said, "Good to see you're feeling better."

Miles laughed and shook his head. "I told the doctor I wanted to go home, but he insisted I stay the night."

"No sense taking chances. I'm glad you're feeling okay," he said and wheeled him into the room, where Mia was patiently waiting.

"You're looking well," Mia said when they entered and Miles scooted up from the wheelchair into the bed, one hand tucked behind him to keep the hospital gown in place.

"Thanks. I can't wait to get out of here," Miles said and pulled the sheets up to his midsection.

"I guess we can come get you in the morning," Mia said, surprising John given their earlier silence in the car. He hadn't figured she'd help him because of their argument.

"I'll be waiting for you first thing," Miles said and looked from Mia to John and back to Mia. Jerking his finger between them, he said, "The two of you—"

"Just friends," Mia said with a wave of her hands.

Friend-zoned, which John hadn't expected, so he supposed he was lucky to have that at least. But it also reminded him of the reason she was here with him in the first place.

"That was a brave thing you did," John said, recalling the moment when his brother had rushed out to tackle their intruder.

Miles shrugged. "I had to do it, bro. I couldn't let him get to you."

John narrowed his gaze as he considered that comment, but Mia beat him to the next question.

"Why do you think he wanted to get to John?" she asked, gaze narrowed as she peered at Miles.

Another careless shrug came as Miles frowned. "Why would they want me? I'm nobody important."

John didn't fail to miss the bitterness there. It wasn't the first time that he'd heard it, but given the prediction the software had made earlier, that tone took on an entirely new meaning.

"You are important, Miles. You're a valued member of the team and you're my brother," John said, hoping to reassure him.

"Right," Miles said, but he was clearly unconvinced.

He quickly added, "I'm feeling a little tired. Would you mind going?"

"Sure. We understand," John said, although he didn't. He'd always looked up to Miles and kept him close. He'd brought him into the company and given him a leadership role even though he'd lacked the experience. On a personal level, he'd done whatever Miles had wanted, from the parties to the Lamborghini. What more could Miles want?

Respect, maybe? was the answer that came immediately. Could that be the reason for what the software had suggested?

"I'd say a penny for your thoughts, only I suspect they're a lot more costly," Mia said as they stepped onto the elevator.

"They are. You could say it's a multimillion-dollar question," he said and shook his head.

"Your software could be wrong, you know," Mia said and as the elevator door opened, she slipped her arm through his and they stepped out to find one of the local news reporters waiting for them in the lobby.

"Mr. Wilson. Is it true someone attacked your offices earlier today?" the young woman said as she chased after them, notebook in hand.

When they hurried past her without answering, she added, "Ms. Gonzalez. Has your family been engaged by Mr. Wilson or is this a personal relationship?"

John glanced at Mia from the corner of his eye, and in response, she brushed a kiss across his cheek and whispered, "Ignore her. She has no right to invade our personal lives."

The reporter was tenacious, however, and followed

them out of the hospital, chasing after them in their dash to his car. To make a quick getaway, he hit the button for the remote start.

A fireball erupted, lifting the body of the Lamborghini into the air.

John threw himself in front of the two women as the force of the blast, the heat of it, threw them back against the doors of the hospital. Bits and pieces of metal and glass rained down on them. The chassis of the car hit the ground in flames with a resounding crash.

His ears were ringing from the concussion of the blast and the nearby car alarms blaring their complaints into the air. Luckily, most of the debris had seemed to go upward and not at them.

He helped Mia to her feet. "Are you hurt?" he said and could barely hear his own voice from the alarms and ringing in his ears. He realized there were also alarms going off inside the hospital and that the fire from his car was quickly spreading to other nearby vehicles.

"I'm okay," she said, the sound muffled to his ears.

Facing the reporter, he inspected her, but she seemed fine, if a little dazed. Still, he asked, "Are you okay?"

The reporter nodded and, not missing a beat, she said, "Can I get a comment from you now?"

TREY HUGGED HER so hard that she worried he might crack a rib. "Trey, I'm okay. Really," Mia said and wiggled to get some breathing room.

Her brother finally released her and jammed his hands on his hips as he inspected the mess in the hospital parking lot.

Mia tracked his gaze to where two firetrucks and assorted firefighters were pouring water on the remains of the Lamborghini and the other cars that had surrounded it. Off to the side, two patrol cars sat at the curb next to a fire marshal's truck and a CSI van.

Mia and the reporter had already provided what little information they could to the police officers. It hadn't been much. Only that John had hit his remote start button, triggering the explosion. Since his car had caused the conflagration, John was still with the police, answering even more questions.

As if reading her thoughts, Trey said, "The bomber probably didn't count on John doing a remote start. Thank God, he did."

Her insides chilled at his comment. If John hadn't done that, the two of them would be dead right now. The reporter, too, if she had continued to dog after them. Her determination had probably saved them since it had pushed John to start the car before they got anywhere near it. But even as she thought that, another idea took hold and refused to leave.

"This wasn't intended for John, was it?" she said, voice choked with fear and emotion.

Trey wrapped an arm around her shoulders and drew her tight to his side. "If it was intended for you, someone is tracking you and brazen enough to plant the bomb right here in the parking lot. But no matter who it was directed at, we'll find a way to keep you safe."

She wanted to believe that, but only luck had saved them tonight. She had never been one to solely rely on luck.

Before she had a chance to reply, an unmarked car

with lights flashing jerked to the curb in front of them. Roni rushed out of the car and up to them.

She hugged Mia hard. "Thank God. When I heard the news, I had to come over and make sure you were okay."

"I'm okay, *amiga*. Shook up. Scared, but okay," she admitted to her best friend.

Roni glanced up at her fiancée. "Have you had a chance to talk to anyone about what they have so far?"

Trey shook his head. "Not yet. Now that you're here, maybe you can go over while I take Mia and John home."

"That's a good idea. They'll probably be more willing to talk to me since you're 'retired,'" Roni said, air quotes reminding him that he was no longer officially one of the men in blue.

"Stay safe and watch your six, *mi amor*. I'm worried this attack was directed at the family," Trey warned and dropped a kiss on Roni's cheek.

"You, too," Roni said and marched toward the first responders while John walked to join her and Trey. But before John could reach them, Miles came running out of the hospital, fully dressed, and raced to his brother's side. He hugged him hard, and John returned the embrace.

Mia and Trey shared a look and together they hurried over to where the two brothers stood.

"I heard about the explosion, and they couldn't keep me inside. I had to make sure you weren't hurt," Miles said and kept an arm around John's shoulders.

"I'm fine. We're fine," he said and shot a look at Mia.

"Right. Mia. You're safe, too," Miles said, almost as an afterthought. It made her wonder if he'd truly forgotten she had been with John, or if there was another reason, like jealousy.

Over the course of their few dates, if you could call them that, she'd gotten the sense that Miles almost resented the attention that John had been paying to her even though Miles had been the one pushing them together at first.

"I am, thank you. But you really should stay the night to make sure you're fine," she said and gestured toward the hospital.

Miles shook his head. "No. I'm AMA and staying that way," he said, referring to his decision to leave against medical advice.

"We can take you home," Trey said and whipped out his phone to call for the SBS Suburban that had brought him to the hospital.

Miles peered all around them, as if searching for something, and then gestured toward the twisted and soaked mess of steel many yards away. "Oh, no. Please tell me that's not the Lambo."

"It's the Lambo," John said and didn't seem quite as upset about it as Miles was.

"Like I said. We'll drive you home," Trey said as the Suburban pulled up to the curb.

They all piled in and once they were seated, Trey said, "Where can we drop you off, Miles?"

In the dim light inside the SUV, Miles peered at John, obviously confused. In response, John said, "Mia, Trey and I have some things to go over. You should go home and get some rest. Take tomorrow off as well."

Miles's earlier happiness that his brother was okay dimmed, and a hard set slipped over his features. "Of course. I'm sure the three of you have important things to do."

"What's important is that you get the rest you need. I'll fill you in on things tomorrow," John said and that seemed to mollify his brother, but only a little.

The silence that settled over all of them weighed heavily on Mia. She felt the confusion, worry and tension in that false quiet and it only lifted the slightest bit after John walked Miles to the door of his South Pointe condo building and returned to the SUV.

When he slipped back in and took a seat beside her behind the privacy screen that had been added to the SUV, he said, "You think this had something to do with him?"

Mia shook her head. "No. I'm worried that explosion was meant to take me out. You and anyone else were just collateral damage."

"Luckily there was no collateral damage besides a few other vehicles," Trey added from the seat behind them.

"That explains the change in my life expectancy. Becoming involved with you is the risk," John said and surprised her by cupping her cheek. "I'm not going to let anything happen to you."

She offered him a weak smile. "I'm sorry I got you involved in this."

"Can we keep the pessimism down a bit, please? I'm not ready to buy the farm just yet," Trey said, lightening what had become a maudlin moment.

John shook his head and, while looking at her, he said, "I'm not either. I've still got too many things to appreciate."

Mia ducked her head, his gaze just too intense. His words offered hope for things she wasn't sure were possible. But even though someone had possibly tried to kill her tonight, she wasn't about to roll over and make it easy for them.

She was going to fight them every step of the way.

"Let's go. We've got crimes to solve."

Chapter Seven

He'd expected Wilson to park his fancy car in a less crowded area of the parking lot. That's what a lot of jerks with fancy cars did to avoid door dings. Parking the car close to other vehicles had made it easier for him to hide while he wired the car with the bomb. But he hadn't expected Wilson to use the remote start, something he did because that stupid reporter had been chasing after them.

And since Wilson had parked close to other cars, those vehicles had deflected almost all of the blast upward, keeping Wilson, Mia and the reporter from being injured.

He raised the binoculars and peered down at the smoking remains of the Lamborghini and the vehicles surrounding it. Firefighters were still pouring water to douse the last of the flames and hopefully the water would wash away a lot of evidence as well.

Not that he'd been careless. He'd been gloved when he'd built the bomb and when he'd connected it to the spare wires he'd installed when the car had been in the repair shop a week earlier. A real shame to lose the car. Now there were only four of them left and way too many of the Gonzalez family. He'd been patiently watching

Wilson in the hopes that Mia would be with him when the car exploded.

They'd been lucky this time. He vowed to make sure they wouldn't be as lucky the next.

"I CAN'T SOLVE crimes on an empty stomach. Besides, I want to hear what Roni has to report from her talks with the local LEOs, fire marshal, and the CSI unit," Trey said and picked up one of the menus Mia had laid out on the table earlier that night. They had all decided on a late dinner, which had enabled John and Mia to visit Miles.

Before getting to know Trey, John might have doubted the sanity of his actions considering all that had happened that day. But a break for food and rest might help all of them get some distance from the events and think more clearly.

Especially since things were getting so convoluted and intertwined. Mia might think that the car bomb—he had no doubt that's what it was—had been intended to take her out, but the bomb had been placed in *his* car when they'd gone to visit *his* brother.

Coincidence or more? he thought.

Mia handed him one of the menus. "I know you like Cubanos."

His gaze met hers and he realized that like her brother, she was trying to draw him out of his thoughts about all that had happened that day. The attack on the office. The bomb at the hospital. *What else could come next?* he wondered.

"Thanks, but I suspect you're probably tired of eating those," he said with a chuckle.

She shook her head. "Never, but a change of pace might be nice."

He handed her back the menu for the Cuban restaurant. "Whatever you'd like, Mia. To be honest, I'm not really hungry."

"I get it, but trying to keep some routines normal helps," Mia said, reached across the table to grab a few more of the menus, and handed them to him.

"Got it," he said with a nod just as Mia's brother Ricky and his fiancée, Mariela, hurried through the door of the conference room.

"We got here as soon as we could," Ricky said and hugged Trey, Sophie and Robbie. There was no mistaking that he was Trey's brother, since they looked alike, but Ricky had a lean runner's build while Trey was slightly taller and more muscular.

Ricky's fiancée was a beautiful woman, with sun-streaked caramel hair, emerald eyes and a voluptuous, centerfold body.

Like Ricky, she hugged her future relatives and then the couple worked their way over to Mia.

When Ricky reached her, he embraced Mia tightly and rocked back and forth with her. "I was so worried."

"We're okay," she said and playfully ruffled the thick waves of his mahogany-brown hair.

Ricky nodded, released her and rushed to his side to shake his hand as Mariela hugged Mia. "John. Good to see you again, although I'm sorry it's under these conditions. How are you doing?"

"Okay, considering we came this close to being toast," John said and brought his index finger and thumb together to emphasize his statement.

At his words, Mia's face paled, but she bucked that

fear by pulling her shoulders back and glaring at him. "But we're not toast and we're going to find out who's behind this."

"We are," Trey said and clapped his hands. "Let's get going with dinner. Roni texted to say she'll be here soon."

"Pizza. It'll let us work while we eat," Mia suggested, and when everyone nodded in agreement, she slipped her phone out of a pocket and made the call.

Barely fifteen minutes had gone as they got settled around the conference room when a ding sounded from Trey's phone. He took a quick look at it, did a little nod and then swiped his screen. With a look at Sophie and Robbie, who were stationed at their laptops at the conference-room table, he said, "Local PD just sent over some videos from the hospital's CCTVs. I just forwarded them to you."

"We'll see what we can do with them," Sophie said.

Robbie nodded in agreement and said, "They might need enhancement, but hopefully we can make them clear enough to compare them with the videos from the drive-by shootings."

"Would you mind sharing them with me?" John asked as Mia sat beside him.

She glanced at him. "Do you think your program can get something from them?"

He nodded. "We've already linked both those drive-bys and believe they're connected to your family. I can analyze if it's the same individual involved."

Mia lifted a perfectly plucked eyebrow. "And if it is?"

"If it is, it's worrisome," Ricky said, a dark glower on his face.

"Why do you say that?" Mariela asked from beside him and grasped his hand, as if to comfort him.

Ricky shook his head and blew out a breath. "These other attacks… They were more personal. They targeted the family for the most part. This one… He could have taken out a lot more people. Innocent people."

"But why our family? That's the key to finding this person. And let's not forget we have to figure out who's trying to steal John's code," Trey said.

John nodded. "I appreciate that, but no one's tried to kill me."

"What about today in the office?" Mia said, surprised by his comment.

With a shrug, he said, "That attack rubs me all wrong."

Mia narrowed her gaze. "You think it was planned to do something else."

"I do. Probably to throw us off the scent. To make us think someone else is behind the hack, when it's really someone in-house," he explained.

"Did your software tell you that?" Trey asked.

John pointed to his midsection. "My gut tells me and you more than most know how important that is. You thought there was something wrong with the attacks and Mariela's ex's death."

That seemed to shock the young woman, who sat up in her seat and opened her eyes wide to look at him. "What do you mean?"

"I'm sorry, Mariela. We meant to talk to you beforehand, but I've always thought there was something off about Jorge's supposed suicide. It just tied things up way too neatly," Trey explained.

"I'm sorry, too. I didn't mean to spring it on you like

that," John said, feeling awful about Mariela's shocked and pained reaction.

"You think Jorge was murdered?" she said in a choked whisper and laid a shaky hand at her throat.

Trey nodded. "I do and I always suspected that it was someone who was trying to hide other crimes, like the drive-bys. Possibly the bombing of Jorge's construction site now that I think about it. Two bombs is just too much coincidence."

"Which means you have someone skilled with weapons and bomb-building. Who would have those kinds of skills?" Mia asked.

"Normally I'd say someone in law enforcement or the military," Trey said and stood as the sound of activity in the lobby area grabbed his attention.

He was going into fight mode, John guessed, but Trey immediately relaxed as Roni waltzed through the conference room door carrying four pizza boxes.

"A little help here," she called out and Trey rushed over to grab the boxes and take them over to a credenza on one side of the conference room.

Roni walked with him and once he'd put down the boxes, she embraced him and Trey slipped his arms around her. They kissed and John had to look away because the obvious love there, and the possibility it might be lost before it could grow, was too painful.

He busied himself by reaching into the knapsack sitting at his feet and pulling out his laptop. "You'll give me access to those videos?" he asked Sophie and Robbie.

Robbie nodded. "Just finished uploading all of them to our cloud server. I'll email you a link so you can get them."

"Thanks," John said, then checked his email and followed the link to the videos.

"Can I get you some pizza?" Mia asked.

"Thanks. I'd appreciate that," he said with a smile, before immersing himself in analyzing the videos.

FEELING USELESS, Mia turned her attention to setting out the various pizza boxes on the credenza, and with Mariela's help, they raided the office pantry for plates, cups, napkins and sodas from the supply they kept for SBS employees.

They returned with them to the conference room to find Robbie flipping open box tops to check the pizza selections.

"Don't worry. I got you your Hawaiian pizza," Mia said with a chuckle and shake of her head. Arms full of the paper goods, she dropped them on the free space on the credenza while Mariela wheeled over a cart with assorted sodas, snugged it close to the furniture and then returned to the table to sit beside Ricky.

Robbie rubbed his hands together with glee, grabbed a plate and snagged a couple of slices of his favorite pizza. Then he prepped a second plate, probably for Sophie. As he started to walk away, Mia shoved napkins against his chest, feeling way too much like a mom even though Robbie was the same age as her.

Trey and Roni walked over next and loaded their plates before returning to the table where Ricky and Mariela were sitting, heads tucked close. Mariela's distress was impossible to miss, and Mia understood. It had been a shock that her ex had possibly been murdered and hadn't committed suicide.

Sophie was just a few feet away, head buried in her

laptop as she worked on the videos that had been sent over by the police department. Robbie laid a plate beside her, and she glanced up and offered her older brother a grateful smile.

Sophie often lost herself in her work, much like John, Mia thought as she glanced back at him. He had his game face on—his brow was creased and his hazel gaze was focused on his laptop.

It yanked a smile to her face since it reminded her of how intense he'd been when they'd been gaming in his penthouse at the Del Sol. She'd been surprised when that was all that he'd wanted when he'd first invited her to come into his private area in the penthouse. She'd worried he'd ask for more, which she had not been prepared to give, and had been determined to find out something—actually anything—about the reclusive multimillionaire.

She hadn't found out much. John Wilson was very much a closed book about his past.

It had intrigued her even more, but also saddened her because it was impossible to miss there was hurt buried there. Hurt that had shaped him, but also kept him from moving on, she suspected.

She muttered a curse since she'd always been one to bring home injured animals and John was very much that: injured.

Shaking that thought loose from her brain, she grabbed a plate, two slices of pizza, a diet soda and a napkin, and took it over to him.

He immediately looked up and smiled. "Thank you. You didn't have to do that."

With a quick lift of her shoulders, she said, "Have to do something. I'm feeling a little…"

"Challenged?" he said sympathetically with a half smile when she struggled for a word.

"Thanks for that," she said and glanced at his laptop, which was running a video while a program shot all kinds of weird lines, dots and numbers across the image.

She pointed to the screen. "What's it doing?"

He jerked his head in the direction of the credenza. "Why don't you get some food and I'll explain."

With a nod, she did as he asked and grabbed herself a couple of slices, since she was feeling famished, and a regular soda because she'd never acquired a taste for the fake stuff. When she returned to sit beside him, he gestured to his laptop.

"Those lines and things are my program doing an analysis of the person in the image. Hopefully it'll be able to tell us his approximate size and weight," John informed her.

"They're grainy, aren't they?" she said and took a bite of a slice.

"They are. Makes it hard to identify features like race and eye color. But you can tell other things."

"Like age? No senior citizen is going to be able to hop up on the edge of the car window like that," she said and circled her finger over the image of the shooter from one of the drive-by videos.

"And he's right-handed," she added as she examined the photo.

"He is. You're very observant. You were able to tell the police a lot about the man who attacked the office earlier," he said.

She did a slight lift of her shoulders. "Like I said, I've hung out with Trey too much. Roni, too. She's a great cop."

"I heard that," Roni teased from across the way, a bright smile on her face.

"Super cop that you are, do you have anything for us from your fellow LEOs at the hospital?" Mia teased right back.

"I do. CSI was able to find some bomb pieces and I asked them to compare those pieces and the explosive used to the bombing at the construction site. ATF is probably going to get involved as well," Roni said.

"Any fingerprints?" Trey asked.

"None so far," Roni said, a frown on her face.

"I'm not a car expert, but aren't the ignition wires under the hood?" Mia said, thinking about her own car and the few times she'd had it serviced.

"Good point. Ignition wires are generally not accessible without lifting the hood," Sophie said and leaned forward to examine her screen. "In this video, he just walks up to the car and slips underneath. He's there for at most a minute or two."

"Which means he had another way to get to the ignition system," Trey said and peered at John. "Have you had the car serviced recently?"

"A little while ago. It was overheating," he said and shook his head. "If he knew that—"

"He's been following you. Maybe because of me. You could have been killed because of me," Mia said and laid a hand against the tightness in her chest.

"But we weren't killed, and he won't get to us again," John said and squeezed her hand to soothe her concerns.

"Can you give us the name of the company that did the servicing? If we're lucky, they'll have CCTVs at their location and we'll be able to get a visual on a suspect," Roni said.

"I should have the info in my emails. I'll send it to you," John said and returned his attention to the laptop.

"What else can you tell us, *mi amor*?" Trey said and got up to grab another slice.

"That I'm the one who should be eating for two, not you," Roni said with a grin and shocked silence filled the room.

Chapter Eight

A second later, a chorus of congratulations erupted from everyone gathered around the table.

"That's wonderful!" Ricky said and hugged his older brother's fiancée. Mariela popped up to hug Roni and Mia did the same, rushing over to embrace her best friend.

"Why didn't you tell me?" she said as she clasped Roni tight.

Roni looked over at Trey as he returned to the table with another slice and accepted a hug from Mariela.

"We only just confirmed it today and with everything that's been going on… We had only told the parents just before Trey got the call about the explosion. We'd talked about when was the right time to tell you—"

"And I guess you decided now was the right time," Trey said facetiously, but bent to drop a kiss on Roni's cheek and Mia hugged him.

Sophie and Robbie got up and walked over as well to congratulate the couple, leaving John sitting there, wondering what to do.

Happy family gatherings had never been a common occurrence in his life, but that was his past and as he glanced across the table at the family gathered there, he realized this was his promise for the future. He pushed away from the table and walked over to shake Trey's hand, and as the women stepped away from Roni, offered his hand to her as well. But Roni hauled him in for a tight embrace.

"Congratulations," he said, his voice slightly hoarse from the emotion he was feeling.

"Thank you, John," she said and as she released him, she whispered, "Treat Mia right."

He nodded and hurried back to his laptop, more determined than ever to discover who was behind the attacks on the Gonzalez family. As for his own issues, he'd set them aside for now and would work on them later. It wouldn't be the first time he'd spent late hours on a problem, and it wouldn't be the last.

When he sat, Mia came to his side and said, "Can I get you another slice?"

He glanced at his empty plate. He'd been so involved in what was happening on his laptop that he'd eaten both slices without thinking. Despite that, he was still hungry.

"I'd like that, thanks. Plain, please," he said with a smile.

She returned the smile, ran a hand across his shoulder in a fleeting caress and walked away to get his pizza. He returned to watching his program do the analysis and just as the results came in, Mia returned with his slice and another diet soda.

"Did you find something?" she asked, then sat beside him and nibbled on her pizza.

"Based on the new video info, the program says the probability of it being the same shooter in both drivebys is 90 percent. On top of that, it estimates he was about six-foot-two, and about 180 pounds."

"And he was either white or white Hispanic," Ricky added, having overheard what they were discussing.

"And right-handed, which makes him sound a lot like the man in the office today," Mia chimed in.

It actually did, John thought, recalling what Mia had told the police earlier that day. Too much coincidence, even though the general characteristics of the man were fairly average.

Looking across at Trey and Roni, he said, "Did the police ever get any CCTV footage from the service areas of the other building?"

"Not as far as I know, but I can reach out to them to confirm," Roni said and stepped away from the table to make the calls.

"What else can we see from the videos?" Mia asked from beside him.

"The program's analyzed—"

"I mean us," she said and gestured between them.

"Us. As in we'll look at the videos?" he asked, just to confirm.

"Yes. Let's look at the videos. Maybe we'll see something that will give us a lead," Mia said and pointed at his laptop.

It made sense to give it a shot the old-fashioned way, but not on his smaller laptop screen. With a flip of the hand in the direction of the big television, he said, "Let's watch them on that."

"Mind if I join you?" Trey said.

"Maybe it'll jog something in our memory," Ricky said, and Mariela nodded.

With a few keystrokes, he cast the videos from the first drive-by that had happened in front of the Del Sol hotel while Trey and Roni were investigating the murder of Trey's partner and a human-trafficking ring.

Unfortunately, the driver hadn't exited the vehicle to shoot and had been both masked and gloved. Except for possibly confirming the shooter's height and build, that video didn't provide any new information.

He pulled up the videos snatched from Ricky's video doorbell as well as those from some of his neighbors during the second drive-by.

"Better quality," John said as he brought up the videos. They were much clearer than the grainier ones from the hotel CCTVs.

They ran through the videos and as they finished, Mia said, "Could you rerun it? I thought I saw something."

He nodded and did as she asked and a few seconds later, she said, "Freeze it. There."

She jumped up from her chair and hurried toward the TV, where she bent slightly to view the screen. As she did so, her designer dress lovingly caressed her curves, pulling his mind from anything having to do with the investigation and forcing him to tame his body's reaction to hers.

Pointing to the screen in the general direction of the shooter's right hand, she said, "His shirt rode up his arm. There's something there on his wrist. Can you zoom in?"

John zoomed in, but as he did so, the video grew more and more pixelated. Despite that, when Mia circled one area on the image, it was clear there was something besides shadows in the space she'd identified.

"Is that a tattoo?" he asked, squinting to try and make sense of the shape that was visible.

"I think so," Ricky said, and Mariela echoed her agreement. "Definitely a tattoo."

Turning his head to the side, he tried to figure it out, but couldn't.

"Beads," Mia said and popped up from where she had been peering at the screen. "Rosary beads. I've seen tattoos like that," she said and motioned to her forearm. "The beads start here and wrap down and around. Sometimes the cross is in the person's palm—"

"Or higher up on the forearm," Mariela said.

"What do they mean?" John said, totally unfamiliar with what you did with a rosary.

JOHN WASN'T CATHOLIC, Mia realized and explained. "Rosary beads are used when praying, usually when you're doing penance. You say the Hail Mary to ask for forgiveness for any sins you've committed, but you can also say the rosary for reflection."

"Our attacker is religious?" John said, clearly unable to link someone wanting to commit murder with a religious type.

"Or a gang member. The rosary has become popular with some Latin gangs," Trey added with a disgusted shake of his head at the perversion of the symbolism.

"We have more clues then. The attacker is a Latino and possibly a gang member," Sophie said.

"And the attacks started happening in the last three months. Maybe this person just got out of prison," Roni suggested for consideration and continued. "I'll run that through our databases in the morning and see what I get. We can compare that to the other evidence we've noted, like knowledge of bomb-making and expertise with weapons."

"But the program now says there might be some

connection to John's program. Minimal, but possible," Mia reminded them.

John nodded. "Maybe whoever is behind the hack hired this guy not knowing about the connection to your family?"

"Maybe. I have some friends who are undercover in the gang scene. I'll reach out to them to see what they can say about anyone looking to hire some muscle," Roni said.

"I still have some connections there as well," Trey added.

"Robbie and I will keep on looking at those stock transactions and if John is willing to give us access, maybe we can look at the server activity to see if someone left any fingerprints that will lead us to them," Sophie said.

"Fingerprints?" Mia asked, eyeing her cousin in puzzlement.

With a shrug, Sophie said, "Hackers use certain things to try to break in. It may give us an idea of how sophisticated they are."

"And we can look at security policies and other things to see if access was changed," Robbie added.

"That makes sense. With all that's happening, I haven't really had a chance to delve into any possible hack, just to try and prevent it again," John explained.

"I can see Roni's getting a little tired, so maybe it's time for us all to go our separate ways and work on all these things," Trey said, but then pointed to her and John. "Except for you two. Someone is clearly out for you so it may be best for you to stay in the penthouse suite. At least for tonight."

John tossed his hands up in the air. "I hadn't planned on that."

"Me either," she said and smoothed her now very wrinkled dress.

"There is some new clothing up there for emergencies like that. Roni can bring you some things in the morning and if you don't mind, John, let me have your house keys. I can check it out and arrange for security there and pick up some clothes for you," Trey said, his tone making it clear that disagreement would not be permitted.

"Yes, sir," Mia said with a salute and a smile. Trey only wanted what was safest for them, but she worried about him and the rest of her family.

Trey seemed to have read her thoughts. "Roni and I can take care of ourselves. Ricky and Mariela are still with *Mami* and *Papi* and it will be hard to get past the security guard at the gate. Same for Sophie and Robbie's condo building, with its doorman and security systems."

John reached for his knapsack, pulled out his keys and tossed them to Trey. "I'll text you the code for my security system."

Trey nodded. "I'm sure it's a good one, but I may beef it up with some other things, if that's okay."

John nodded. "It's okay. Whatever you think we need to keep Mia and me safe."

Mia and me? *Did I hear that right*? Mia wondered, but as she met his gaze, it was obvious she'd heard correctly.

Somehow that didn't bother her. With every hour that she spent with him, she was growing more and more intrigued by him, attracted to him.

Trey looked her way and when she didn't protest, he nodded. "We'll be going then. See you in the morning."

"Carolina is supposed to be back tomorrow, but I think I should call her and let her know that she and *Tia* Elena should extend their girls' getaway," Mia said.

"I think that's a great idea," Trey confirmed and then he and Roni rose as one, followed by Ricky and Mariela. They came over to hug her and John, and then went to Sophie and Robbie, who were still sitting in front of their laptops.

At a questioning lift of Trey's brow, Robbie said, "We're just going to work a little longer."

"Not too long," Sophie said, which was unusual since she was the one who usually lost track of time when she was on the computer.

With a nod, the two couples walked out, leaving her with her cousins and John. She pointed up and said, "Let me show you to the penthouse suite."

Chapter Nine

The elevator doors opened into a luxuriously appointed penthouse suite.

John strolled in, the weight of his knapsack seeming heavier than usual. Considering all that had happened that day, he was surprised it didn't drag him to the floor, but having the support of the Gonzalez family had made a world of difference.

Especially Mia. Having her beside him…

He tried not to think of that too much because he didn't want to have to deal with the disappointment. He'd already had too much of that in his life.

"Let me show you to the guest bedroom," she said and flung a hand in the direction of a far wall.

He glanced that way and realized the space had a central living-and-dining-room area with a kitchen off to one side and what looked like another bedroom on the opposite wall. The bedroom he followed her to was the one farthest from the kitchen.

The entire wall opposite the kitchen and a centrally located fireplace was made of glass, providing amazing views of downtown Miami, Miami Beach and the waters beyond.

"You don't need to worry about the glass. Like downstairs, it's all privacy-protected," she explained.

"There should be an assortment of robes and things in the closet and drawers as well as fresh toiletries and towels in the bathroom," she said.

"Do you have overnight guests often?" he asked, wondering why the family would have included such a space in their building.

With a lift of her dainty shoulders, she said, "Occasionally. Usually, people who don't want other people to know they're in the area or need to be safeguarded. Trey and Roni had to stay here during their earlier investigation. More often it's a family member who's working late."

"Like Sophie and Robbie?" he asked, feeling bad that the two tech gurus were still at work downstairs when he had left.

"Like Sophie and Robbie. I don't know how they do it sometimes," Mia admitted with a roll of her blue eyes.

Shrugging, John admitted, "It comes with the territory. I often get so lost in the code that I don't realize I've been at it for hours."

Mia narrowed her gaze and peered at him. "If you want to work on something, why not get comfortable and have at it."

Have at it? No woman had ever said that to him about his programming. What few women he'd ever been involved with had resented the time he'd spent on his laptop while enjoying the financial benefits it brought.

"I think I will. Feel free to turn in if you want to. I imagine you're tired," he said and laid his knapsack on the bed.

"I am but wired, too. Still trying to wrap my head

around all that's happened," she confessed and wrapped her arms around herself, as if trying to keep herself from falling into pieces.

He walked over and cupped her cheek, admiring the strength she had shown. "Weren't you the one who told me we'd figure this out?"

She offered him a fragile smile. "I am."

Her cheek was so soft beneath his thumb, he had to stroke it gently. "Why don't you get comfortable as well. Maybe we can share a drink to relax before I start working."

She nodded and her smile brightened. "I'd like that. I think I'm going to take a shower first."

"Sounds like a great idea. I'll meet you out there," he said and waited until she was out of the room to scrounge through the drawers to find an assortment of comfy T-shirts and sweatpants with the tags still on them.

He grabbed a University of Miami T-shirt and matching sweatpants and headed for a quick shower.

When he exited into the living-room area, he heard the whoosh of the water running in Mia's shower. He opened the refrigerator to see it was fully stocked with an assortment of sodas and food items. The cabinets beside the fridge held plates, glasses and snacks.

He walked to the side of the kitchen where there was a bar with an assortment of liquors and glasses. Remembering what Mia had ordered on a couple of their dates, he popped some ice cubes into highball glasses and added a couple of fingers of a single-malt scotch. After picking up the glasses, he walked with them to the sofa, placed them on the coffee table and, feeling the chill of the air-conditioning, went over to the glass fireplace and lit it.

"Being decadent, are we?" Mia teased as she walked out of the bedroom, fluffing her wet, shoulder-length hair with her hands. Her face was devoid of makeup, but if anything, she was even prettier in her natural state. Her cheeks bore the kiss of the sun, and her skin was flawless even without the benefit of foundation or whatever women put on their faces. Impossibly long lashes framed those amazing blue eyes that could be as bright as the sunniest Miami day, or as deep and blue as the ocean during a storm.

"John?" she asked at his prolonged perusal.

"Yes, being decadent. Not something I'm used to, I must confess," he admitted and handed her a glass as she curled up into the corner of the sofa, tucking her legs beneath her.

Like him, she had slipped into a T-shirt and sweats, making her look like a young coed and not the sophisticated woman he was used to seeing.

"You look…nice," he said, coughed and looked away as he noticed how the chill of the AC had tightened her nipples beneath the soft cotton fabric.

From the corner of his eye, he caught the rush of color up her neck and to her cheeks, and how she untucked her legs and drew up her knees to provide some protection from the chill, or maybe his gaze.

"Silly," he said and flinched as he realized he'd said it aloud.

"It is," she admitted and the color across her cheeks deepened. "I mean, we're both adults. Consenting ones at that. We should be able to deal with being attracted to each other."

He jumped with surprise at that admission. "You're attracted to me."

She muttered a curse beneath her breath and took a bracing swig from her drink. Finally, she said, "I am. But it's not just physical. You're a puzzle."

"Wrapped in an enigma and covered with a paradox," he teased to hopefully get them past the awkwardness of the moment.

She laughed, as he'd hoped she would, and shook her head. "Seriously. We're a pair, aren't we?"

"We are. Tell me about yourself, Mia. Tell me about the girl who didn't have everything," he said, recalling her words from earlier that day.

"I can't say I was like most little girls. Being in the middle of Trey and Ricky was a challenge," she admitted.

John could understand. They were very different men. Trey was an all-action guy while Ricky was quieter and more cerebral, which actually explained a lot about Mia.

"I see now why you can kick ass as good as any marine, as well as fix hurts like you did with Miles," he said.

She chuckled, shook her head and took another sip of her scotch. "I had to learn to survive."

She had not only survived, but she had also probably exceeded her own expectations. "You've done very well for yourself, Mia. I'm sure your family is proud."

She nodded without hesitation. "They are."

He wished he could be as sure of how his family would have felt about him and she seemed to sense his uncertainty. "What about your family? What you've done is amazing."

Peering down at his glass as if it would have the answer, he delayed, unsure of what to say. But then Mia reached over and laid a hand on his, offering comfort.

"It's okay if you don't want to share," she said, her voice husky with emotion much like what he was feeling.

For so long he'd kept it all to himself and it had become the proverbial albatross around his neck, dragging him down. Maybe finally letting it free would lessen that burden.

Slugging down a gulp of scotch, he winced as it burned down his throat. Slowly lifting his gaze, he met hers, the color of a stormy sea, reflecting the pain in his.

"My dad was abusive. He used to beat the heck out of my mom. Miles and me, too, sometimes if we didn't hide fast enough."

She said nothing, only twined her fingers with his to offer support.

"Luckily, and I can't believe I'm using that word to talk about someone dying," he said and shook his head in disbelief. At another gentle squeeze on his hand, he continued. "He was killed in a bar fight. I guess he decided to beat on the wrong person. With him gone, we were safe, but it was really hard on my mom to keep the family going. She had to work long hours so we wouldn't go hungry, but she did it and somehow made sure we could go to college. Unfortunately, she died of cancer right after I graduated."

"That must have been so rough on you—" she paused briefly "—and Miles." And it was obvious she didn't have as much sympathy for his brother as she did for him.

"He's not as bad as you think, Mia. He's always protected me and had my back," John said and took another sip of his scotch.

"I'd be lying to you if I said he didn't rub me the wrong way," Mia said.

"All I ask is that you give him a chance."

A CHANCE? To a man she worried was behind the attempted hack of John's program? But even as she thought that, it occurred to her that she didn't see Miles as being involved in the attempt to kill them. Because of that, and because she wanted to explore whatever this was between her and John, she would do as he asked.

"I will try, John," she said and raised her glass as if in a toast. "To new beginnings."

His smile was carefree as he tapped his glass to hers. "To new beginnings."

They both took a sip of the scotch, but then sat there in companionable silence for long moments until Mia shifted closer and cupped his cheek.

Beneath her palm, his skin was rough with his evening beard. She leaned close and breathed in the scent of him, the eucalyptus-and-mint body wash he had used. "You smell good. Feel good," she said and brushed her lips across his cheek.

He locked his gaze on hers, and being this close, she could see the shards of gold and green in his hazel eyes. See the desire darken the color to an almost molten gold.

He tunneled his hand into the damp strands of her hair, but didn't urge her closer, letting her make the next move.

She didn't hesitate, but she didn't rush either.

Even though they'd gone out a few times before, she'd had her doubts about him. Some of those doubts had disappeared in just a day as she'd seen him deal with all that was happening. How he'd protected her during the office attack and again during the explosion. The admission that the parties and over-the-top car weren't his choices, but his brother's.

Narrowing her gaze, she examined his face. A strong and handsome face.

"I don't know what to make of you," she admitted and stroked his cheek again.

"Do you have to? Can't we just see where this goes?" he said and ran the back of his hand across her cheek, his touch tender. Achingly restrained.

Considering what he'd told her, it occurred to her that maybe he wasn't used to gentleness. Gentleness like what she'd grown up with in her loving and very giving family.

Wanting to give that to him, she shifted the last final inch and kissed him. A soft, fleeting kiss, offering tenderness. Inviting him to take the lead and let her know what he wanted. If he wanted her.

JOHN'S BODY SHOOK as she kissed him, and he barely contained his moan of need.

She smelled so good, tasted even better, he thought as he sampled her mouth with his. The kiss, tentative at first, was growing deeper, needier, when she answered his demand, meeting his mouth with hers over and over, opening her mouth to him and slipping from the corner of the couch to ease into his lap.

Her center cradled his hardness as she straddled him and this time he couldn't hold in his moan. But he tempered his need because it was too soon. Especially with all that had happened that day.

She must have felt his pullback because she sat back on her haunches and peered at him, but she laid her hands on his shoulders and stroked them, the touch gentling. Comforting.

"I know it's maybe too soon for…you know," she said, and a telltale flush swept up across her cheeks.

He loved that for all her sophistication, she could still be flustered about something so basic.

Smiling, he swept his finger across that color. "Too much has happened today and maybe you're vulnerable," he said, earning a roll of her eyes.

"Maybe *I'm* vulnerable," he teased, prompting her to laugh and run a hand through his shower-dampened hair before she leaned forward again.

"Maybe I just want to kiss. Just kiss," she said and did just that, opening her mouth on his.

He kissed her back, took her breath into his as if he needed it to survive. She was life and love and so much more than he'd ever had before. He cradled her back with his hands, keeping her close until the kisses slowed, and they shifted away from each other.

"I like kissing you," she said, grinning, her blue eyes dancing with laughter.

"I like kissing *you*," he said, feeling a lightness in his heart that he'd never felt before and it all had to do with the amazing woman in his arms. A woman who was strong. Caring, and yet had her own hurts as well.

It couldn't have been easy being sandwiched between Trey and Ricky. Surviving those early family hardships to watch them become near legends in Miami. Becoming her own legend and millionaire with her hard work as an influencer. But that only made him remember that someone wanted to hurt her family because of that success, which made him even more determined to find whoever was behind it.

"I won't let anyone hurt you," he said and brushed back a lock of her dark hair that had fallen forward when they kissed.

"*We're* going to stop him and we're going to find out who's trying to steal your software," she said.

He frowned at the mention of his program. "Sometimes I'm sorry I ever wrote it."

She startled a little, surprised. "Why? It seems like it could be really helpful."

"Or really hurtful, like the Manhattan Project. I can't imagine what those scientists thought when they realized how what they had created would be used," he said, once again thinking about how much harm could be done if his software got into the wrong hands.

She cradled his cheek again and then ran her finger across his mouth in a fleeting caress. "We won't let that happen."

It was his warrior speaking and he told himself to believe it because she believed it.

"We won't," he said to convince himself, and with a final kiss, she slipped off his lap and stood.

"Did you want to work at the dining-room table?" she asked and nodded her head in the direction of the dining section of the open-concept room.

He shook his head. "A little tired of sitting at a table. I'll just get my laptop and work here," he said and patted the comfy cushions of the leather sofa.

"Can I make you some coffee?" she said and wrapped an arm across her chest, suddenly uneasy.

"I'd love that." He shot to his feet and went to get his knapsack.

In the bedroom, he heard the distant whir of the coffee machine as it ground the coffee beans and the earthy smell of the brew hit him when he returned to the sofa. The gurgle and hiss of the coffee machine filled the quiet as he unpacked his laptop and power cord, then settled onto the sofa, feet resting on the coffee table.

As he logged on to the network, Sophie's earlier words about fingerprints slammed into his consciousness. She was right that whoever had tried to hack in may have left little clues behind and if it was someone in-house, maybe he could recognize who by how they'd attempted to do the hack. After all, he knew the strengths and weaknesses of each of the programmers he'd kept on after selling his start-up. When looking at a project, he could tell who had coded what section because each of them had a unique way of approaching a program.

It was with that knowledge in mind that he started looking at the security logs and other information available on the servers, as well as on the logs of the desktop computer that he sometimes used.

The desktop computer Miles had been sitting near when John had returned from lunch with Trey the other day.

Thankfully, Mia came over at the moment, snapping him from going to that dark place of distrust with regard to his only remaining family.

"Light and sweet, right?" she said as she placed a mug on a coaster on the coffee table.

"Yes, thanks," he said, but was surprised as she placed a second mug on the table and snuggled into the corner of the couch.

"You don't have to keep me company," he said, guilty that she felt she had to stay.

She smiled, but it was a tired smile. "Not a problem,

plus I have to catch up on some of my own work, too," she said and held up her smartphone.

"Got it." For someone who was likely on social media daily, probably multiple times a day, she'd been too caught up with everything else to post anything. But he trusted that she wouldn't post anything that would compromise their safety.

Focusing on his laptop, he searched for clues as to who had done the hacking, taking sips of his coffee as he did so. He hoped the rush of caffeine and sugar would give him the energy he needed to check the various logs. He went through every line meticulously until his eyes were glazing over with fatigue.

A soft thud drew his attention. Mia's smartphone had fallen to the floor, and she was sound asleep beside him. The barest snore escaped her, dragging a smile to his face.

A quick glance at the clock on his laptop warned it was nearly three in the morning and the day's events had taken their toll on him.

Time for both of them to get some sleep.

He rose and carefully slipped his arms beneath her to carry her to her bedroom. At his touch, she smiled sleepily, wrapped her arms around his neck and tucked her head against his chest.

Grateful for the strength training he had been doing for years, he easily lifted her and carried her into the bedroom, but as he laid her on the bed, she refused to let go.

"Stay with me," she murmured softly.

It would be torture to lie beside her for what little remained of the night, but what pleasant torture. And maybe lying beside her would drive the niggling worry from his head about what the logs might be revealing: that one of the attempted hacks had come from his desktop computer.

He slipped beneath the sheets beside her, and she snuggled into his side, her arm wrapped around his midsection and her head pillowed on his shoulder. That soft snore came again, reminding him that she wasn't perfect.

But maybe perfect for me, he thought as he lay beside her, the weight of her comforting, creating peace to drive away the concerns that had crept into him as he'd searched for those telltale fingerprints.

Fingerprints that were leading him in the direction of someone quite dear to him. Someone he would have trusted with his life. *Had* trusted with his life when his father would go on a rampage.

She stroked her hand across his chest, as if sensing his unrest, and it calmed him.

But as he drifted off, those troubling thoughts tangled into his brain like a noxious weed, digging their roots deep. Warning him that his life might not ever be the same again.

Chapter Ten

Mia woke against the delicious warmth of John's body. She'd gotten a surprisingly good sleep despite going to bed late and rousing when John had carried her to bed.

His presence had helped tame the fear created by all the dangers of the day.

When he sucked in a deep breath and stretched, she shifted upward to drop a quick kiss on his lips.

He awakened more fully and rolled to trap her under him, his body hard against hers. He kissed her more deeply and she responded, savoring the feel of him. Savoring the peacefulness of the morning as the sun was barely cracking the horizon, and the first fingers of purple and pink were creeping over the darker blues of the ocean.

She lay there, enjoying that peace. Embracing the calm that filled her because she sensed today might be trying.

"I don't want to get up," she said with a sigh against his lips.

"I don't either. This just feels…wonderful," he admitted and rolled onto his back once more but kept her close to his side.

She settled in again until the annoying ringtone of

her phone warned that it was time to get up. The phone was still in the living room, and she let the alarm finish its ringing. Its warning chime would come again in ten minutes, interrupting their peace again.

But barely two minutes had gone by when the phone chirped that a call was coming in.

Fearing the worst, she scrambled from the bed and rushed to the coffee table to answer her phone. Trey was calling.

"What's up?" she asked and plopped onto the couch.

"*Papi* and I are at the office. Ricky, Sophie and Robbie are on their way. We thought we might order in breakfast so we can get an early start. Roni has clothes for the two of you if it's okay for her to come up," he said.

She'd been hoping for some quiet time with John that morning before reality intruded. With a sigh of frustration, she said, "It's okay for Roni to come up. I'll let John know."

Trey must have sensed her frustration. "Everything okay?"

"Sure. Why wouldn't it be? I mean, it's not like someone tried to kill us yesterday. Maybe twice," she said facetiously, not ready to face the real world quite yet.

"I get it, *hermanita*. It's not easy to handle this kind of stress on a daily basis," Trey said.

He was only trying to commiserate, but it made her feel incredibly guilty as well, since both Trey and her father had regularly dealt with it, first as cops and then as part of the SBS. It only strengthened her determination to become more involved and help alleviate some of that stress.

"Thank you and *Papi* for all that you do," she said and hung up.

When she looked up, her gaze clouded by tears, John was standing there, peering at her sympathetically. "We can stay here for a little longer if you want."

She shook her head. "No, I'm fine. Roni is on her way with our clothes and I'm sure you have things to share with them."

His features tightened at that mention. "Not much," he said but it was obvious to her he was keeping something from her.

Because she trusted him, she'd let him keep that secret for now.

She bolted to her feet just as the elevator dinged to warn that Roni had arrived. As her friend came off the elevator, Mia hurried over and hugged her hard.

"Thank you and congratulations again, even if you didn't tell me first," she said, rocking Roni from side to side joyfully.

"I wanted to, believe me. We had planned to ask Ricky and you over for dinner, but then we got the call about the explosion, and everything got crazy," Roni said and handed a bag to John. "Trey picked some things up for you."

She handed Mia a second bag. "Casual clothes since I thought you might be running around today."

"Thanks. Are you staying for the meeting?" she asked as Roni walked with her to her bedroom while John went into his to change.

"Only for a little bit. I'm heading into the office to do those searches we discussed last night. Hopefully it will give us a good pool of possible suspects," Roni said and sat on the bed.

Roni placed the small duffel bag on the bedspread and pulled out the clothes her friend had packed for her. Comfortable faded jeans, a short-sleeved light blue blouse, soft fleece hoodie and assorted underthings. Another few changes of clothes and, beneath them, her favorite sneakers.

Mia slipped out of the T-shirt and sweatpants that she'd taken from the guest supplies and left them on the bed for their housekeeping staff to launder. As she slipped into her underthings and socks, she said, "Do you really think someone is targeting SBS?"

Roni shrugged uneasily and dipped her head. "When Trey first told me his concerns, I had my doubts, but now…"

Now those doubts were gone, Mia thought as she stepped into her jeans and tugged them up. They were buttery soft against her skin and sat low on her hips. The blouse hung loosely around her midsection and just kissed the waistband of the jeans. She wasted no time slipping on her sneakers and grabbed the hoodie.

Facing her friend, she said, "Thank you again for bringing this."

"What are friends for?" Roni said with a smile and stood.

Mia hugged her friend hard. "I'm so happy for you and Trey."

Roni's smile grew even broader. "I'm happy, too."

Mia slipped her arm through Roni's. As they walked toward the door, Roni said, "What's happening with you and Wilson?"

"He's a good kisser," Mia said with a laugh.

With the arch of an eyebrow, Roni said, "A good kisser, huh? Is it serious?"

Mia pursed her lips and shrugged. "Is it serious? I can't say. Could it be serious? Maybe," she admitted.

"Fair enough," Roni said, and Mia stopped short, surprised by her friend's response.

"Really? That's all you've got to say?" Mia asked, staring at her.

With a hunch of her shoulders, Roni said, "I spent a little time with him during an investigation. I didn't know what to make of him at first, but once I got to know him, he seemed like a nice guy."

A nice guy. Mia couldn't deny that, but was it enough?

Mr. Nice Guy was waiting for them out in the living room, his ever-present knapsack slung over his shoulder. Like her, he was dressed casually in a pale yellow, linen *guayabera* and faded jeans. His feet were clad in brightly colored sneakers that made her think of the boyish side of him that often emerged when he was video gaming.

The sneakers dragged a smile to her lips and invited her to go over and drop a kiss on his lips, not fazed by the fact that Roni was there to witness it.

John seemed a little taken aback by the openness of the affection and gazed between her and Roni, who said nothing about it.

"Let's go," Mia said and hurried to the elevator.

JOHN WAITED FOR the two women to enter the conference room, where the South Beach Security patriarch, Ramon, stood chatting with his two sons. Ramon's head was downcast as he listened to something Ricky was saying while Trey was immobile, arms across his chest, a stern set to his face.

Ricky stopped talking as they walked in, and Ramon and Trey looked their way. The hardness on Trey's face melted away as he caught sight of his fiancée and he smiled and walked over to greet them.

"Good morning," Trey said as he shook his hand, then hugged the two women.

Ramon and Ricky both came over and greeted them, but it was impossible for John to miss that Ramon remained troubled by whatever Ricky had been sharing earlier.

"I should get going and run those searches. I'll send the information over as soon as I have anything," Roni said, then hugged Mia and Trey, and kissed them both before rushing out the door.

Ramon swept a hand in the direction of the credenza, where an assortment of breakfast pastries, bagels and spreads sat along with carafes with a trio of juices, coffee and tea. Creamers and sweeteners completed the breakfast offerings.

"Please help yourselves while we wait for Sophie and Robbie. They'll be here in a few minutes," Ramon said.

"Thank you," John said, hungry despite his concerns about what they would do today to stop the possible attacks on the Gonzalez family and the theft of his program.

He apparently wasn't the only one since Mia was immediately at his side, following his lead as he grabbed a bagel and cream cheese and prepped himself a coffee.

By the time he sat down at the table, with Mia at his side, Sophie and Robbie were walking in and setting up their laptops to work.

"Good morning," Sophie said with a smile, looking none the worse for wear even though she and Robbie had stayed late the night before.

Robbie echoed her greeting and while the two of them went over to get breakfast, Trey took control of the meeting.

He stood to the right of his father, who was at the head of the table, leaned his hands on the top edge of one of the executive leather chairs and began. "As promised, I reached out to some friends for information on what's happening with local gangs. There were rumors a couple of weeks ago that someone was looking to hire a gang member to put the hurt on someone."

"And you think that gang member attacked my brother in our office?" John said, trying to wrap his head around Trey's report.

"It seems probable, which is why your program somehow made the connection between your possible hack and the attempts on the SBS," Sophie said.

But there was something niggling in his brain. "Someone in my office paid for that attack to either have time to steal something—"

"Or to hide something," Mia said, repeating the idea that had been tossed out the day before.

The attack played out in his mind from the moment the intruder had rushed in, to the short minutes when Miles had fought off the man. Shaking his head, he said, "Most people were standing at their office doors, shocked by what was happening."

From the corner of his eye, he caught how Mia's hand shook as she put down her cup of coffee. She was upset, holding back, and he suspected why.

"No one would have been in a position to steal anything during the attack," Robbie said.

"No," he answered without hesitation and met Trey's gaze. He was clearly troubled, his blue-green gaze as turbulent as the ocean during a hurricane.

"Eliminating theft, that leaves deception, and the most likely suspect would be whoever is trying to hack your software. They used the attack to hide what they're doing or mislead anyone investigating the hack," Trey said.

"He wanted to throw off any suspicion that might come his way," John said, and it was impossible not to run with that thought, especially after the research he had done the night before. "He paid a gang member to do the attack. Stood by as it happened or maybe even tried to be a hero."

His hands tightened into fists of rage, not wanting to believe Miles had had a hand in it, but as someone who dealt with logic all the time…

"Occam's razor. The simplest explanation is usually the right one," Mia whispered from beside him.

"You remembered that," he said, recalling one of their dinner dates and how he'd tried to explain to her how he developed some of his ideas.

"I did, but maybe this isn't one of those times," she said and laid her hand over one of his clenched fists.

"But Miles *is* the simplest explanation," he finally said aloud.

"If he's the one who has access to your desktop," Sophie chimed in and shot a quick look at Robbie to continue.

"Our search of the logs and other things shows some unexpected activity coming from that computer, but also a small DDoS attack—"

"Denial-of-service. An attacker will create excessive traffic on a website or server to overwhelm it. I noticed the increased traffic when I did my first review, but it didn't seem to last long enough," John explained to Mia.

"It didn't," Sophie confirmed and continued. "Whoever tried it was either worried they hadn't hid their trail enough or didn't really know how to execute the DDoS."

"Or maybe they had second thoughts. Maybe they felt guilty about doing it," Mia suggested.

John wanted to believe that was the reason. That Miles had had second thoughts, maybe even about the attack if he was behind it. *Had that been the reason he'd rushed the intruder to stop him*? he wondered.

"That kind of guilt is possible," Ricky said from across the room and peered at Trey, who nodded, prompting him to go on.

"Trey asked me to do a possible profile on who might be responsible for the attacks on the family, but first let's discuss whoever paid for this gang member. You're right that they might be experiencing guilt, especially if they had felt loyalty to you, John."

"Like one of my employees?" John asked.

"Like one of them. I'm assuming you've made them all quite well off. You trusted them enough to go with you on this new start-up—"

"Or left them behind. Isn't it possible it's someone who resents not being asked to join the new start-up?" Mia suggested.

John appreciated that she was playing devil's advocate even though he was well aware of her dislike of Miles.

"Someone that I left behind would have been capable of executing a DDoS. Whoever did this wasn't a sophisticated hacker," he said.

"Like Miles?" Trey said, arching a dark eyebrow.

"Like Miles," John finally admitted out loud as he relaxed his fists, the admission washing away his rage and replacing it with sadness. Mia immediately slipped her hand into his, offering comfort.

"We can make that assumption, but let's not rule out other possibilities," Ramon warned from the head of the table.

"*Papi* is right. We have to keep all options open to not avoid missing something," Trey said.

"Like the fact that the gang member knew when you would be there," Sophie said and held out her hand. "Please let me have your cell phone."

Puzzled, he said, "I already checked it when I first thought there was a hack."

Despite that, he unlocked it with his fingerprint and handed it to her. It took her only a few swipes, then she said, "The locate function was enabled the night before the attack. Who had access to your phone?"

Miles did during dinner, he thought, and while he didn't say it, everyone around the table knew who might have possibly done it.

"I don't know why Miles would do something like that or why someone wants to attack your family," he said, trying to divert attention away from his brother while he wrapped his head around Miles's possible betrayal.

"Whoever it is may see a family that he believes did something wrong that warrants punishment," Ricky said.

"Like what? We try to help people," Mia said in defense of the Gonzalez family members.

"But maybe someone thinks we didn't do enough or did too much or accused one of their loved ones," Ricky pointed out.

"If it is a gang member, he could have a gripe if I

helped arrest a fellow gang member," Trey said with a dejected drop of his shoulders, as if burdened by guilt.

"Not just you, Trey," Mia said quickly, also sensing her brother's change of mood.

Trey shook his head and blew out a disgusted sigh as Ricky said, "Mia's right, Trey. It could be any of the cases we've worked on with the SBS."

Trey nodded, but it was obvious he wasn't convinced. "Maybe we'll be able to find out more once Roni sends over a list of recently released gang members."

Ricky peered at John and said, "The person trying to steal your code… It could be just simple theft motivated by greed."

John didn't fail to hear what Ricky was implying. "But it also could be more."

With a shrug, Ricky continued. "It could be someone who's jealous of what you've accomplished, resents it, or feels they're not getting enough credit for what they do."

Once again, the warning bells were going in his head that Miles fit those criteria. "Miles resents that I don't let him make important decisions at the company," John admitted.

"But you let him do a lot of things for you," Mia said, trying to be supportive.

"I do, but…it's because I feel guilty," he said and tapped at a spot above his heart. "I feel guilty because he always protected me, and I feel like I owe him for that."

"If he senses that guilt, it could make him even more resentful, John," Ricky said, his tone filled with compassion and not condemnation.

John nodded. For too long he'd wanted to clear the air with Miles, tell him how he felt. But he'd worried about how Miles would react. Worried that he'd lose the only family he had.

"Maybe it's time to talk to him," Mia said with a tender squeeze of his hand and a reassuring smile.

With another nod, John said, "Maybe." He shot a quick look at his watch and said, "If there isn't more right now, I should really go down and make sure my employees are okay. Get to work on trying to find out more about that DDoS and the other hacks."

"We'll keep working on that as well," Sophie said.

"That makes sense, John. We can reconvene once I have Roni's info and have a chance to review it," Trey said.

"Great," John said and shot to his feet, and Mia joined him.

At his questioning look, she offered him another smile and said, "I can help you unpack. I'm good at unpacking. Just ask Trey."

Her older brother chuckled and shook his head. "She is, John. I'd take her up on it unless you want boxes sitting in your office for weeks."

John peered at him and then Mia. Seeing they were determined, he nodded. "I'd appreciate the help."

Chapter Eleven

He laid the tripod for the rifle on the coping along the roof of the skyscraper and peered through the scope toward the South Beach Security building.

The glass sides of the building gleamed aqua in the bright morning sun, reflecting the almost blinding rays and the silhouettes of the nearby structures.

He knew where the family hid in the building. The two floors where they housed their business, John Wilson's start-up on the floor below the SBS and the penthouse suite.

Focusing on those floors with the scope, he tried to see through the glass, but the film on the windows made it impossible.

Luckily, he'd planned for that option and had slipped an AirTag into Miles Wilson's knapsack. Pulling out his phone, he went to his cloud account for the location information. The tracker was working just fine. Miles wouldn't even know he was being tracked since he was using an Android phone, but he only had three days before the provider might fry the device for suspicious behavior.

Based on the tracker's signal, Miles was right in front

of the building. He turned the scope in the direction indicated by the signal and, sure enough, there he was.

He watched as Wilson walked into the building. He guessed it would only take a few minutes to clear security, get an elevator and reach the floor for the start-up. Would Miles drop his knapsack in his office and head for a coffee? If he did, it would be a waste of time for him to be up here.

But if he went straight to the boss's office…

Mɪᴀ ᴘʟᴀᴄᴇᴅ ᴛʜᴇ box on John's desk while he unloaded an assortment of books into a bookshelf at the far side of the room. Being a tech guy, she hadn't expected him to have so many physical books, but there were at least two boxes of them on diverse subjects. She itched to go over and see which ones in the hope they would reveal even more about the man who was increasingly owning a bigger piece of her heart.

She unloaded the first of the items from the box: a red stapler. Laughing, she laid it to the side as she took out the rest of the desktop accessories. She'd leave the placement of everything to John because the layout of the desk was such a personal thing.

She was about to walk over to the bookcase to help John when Miles walked into the room, his knapsack slung over his shoulder. He dipped his head in greeting and then sauntered to John's side. As they stood there, it was impossible to deny they were related, but John was slightly taller and leaner. John's hair was wavy, and more brown than blond, unlike Miles, who had a high fade haircut where the longer strands were ruthlessly gelled into place.

"How's it going?" Miles said and let his knapsack slip to the ground, as if he intended to stay for a while.

A *plink*, like that of two marbles colliding, made her half turn toward the window. A slight crack in the window confused her until the *plink* came again. Suddenly a hole appeared in the glass and needles of pain erupted in the hand she had leaned on the desk.

Stunned, she froze, but a second later John rushed at her, wrapped his arms around her and hauled her around the protection of the desk, drawing her down beside him.

In a burst of motion, Miles joined them as shot after shot broke through the skyscraper's glass wall and slammed into the heavy wood of the desk.

John whipped out his smartphone, but Mia stayed his hand. It was then she noticed the blood on her hand and the splinters from the wood of the desk. "Call Trey. Maybe he can get eyes on whoever is firing at us."

"Are you crazy! Dial 911, John," Miles said as he cowered beside them. With each bullet slamming into the wood, he jumped, and all color had fled from his face.

John called Trey, who immediately answered. "Someone's shooting at us. We're pinned down in my new office."

"Stay down. I'm calling 911," Trey said and hung up.

A salvo of shots hit the desk and then silence. Blessed silence.

Mia released a sharp breath of relief and melted against the back of the desk. Her body was shaking from the adrenaline rush and John wrapped her in his arms.

"It's over," he said and kissed her temple.

This incident was over, but the threat to them, all of

them… It was still there and just as deadly as John's program had predicted.

"You're hurt. We need to take care of your hand," John said and started to rise, but she urged him to stay down.

"We need to wait for the all-clear from Trey," she said.

Miles said, "I'm not going to be a sitting duck here." He got on all fours and crawled out of the office and into the hallway.

When Miles had gone, she said, "How did someone know we were here?"

"We'll figure it out, Mia. The most important thing now is to make sure we're all safe," John said.

A second later, John's phone rang. "Trey," he said and put the call on speaker.

"Are you all okay?"

Mia waved her uninjured hand to stop him because Trey would lose it if he knew she was hurt.

John understood and said, "We're okay. Is it safe?"

"It's safe. Police chopper caught sight of someone on a roof two buildings over. They lost him when he used the rooftop access to enter the building. Officers are headed there now. They're coming here, too. I'll be down in a couple of minutes."

"We'll be waiting for you," John said and ended the call.

He held his hand out to her. "Let's get out of here and tend to your hand."

She rose on shaky legs, wobbly until John slipped an arm around her waist to offer support.

He walked her toward a conference room where the windows faced in a different direction. Miles was at the front desk, standing by Rachel, who was on the phone, presumably with the police.

"Are you okay?" Miles asked and ran a hand through his hair, creating sharp, erratic spikes in the strands.

"Can you track down a first-aid kit? Mia's hand needs some cleaning and patching," John said.

Mia looked down at her hand where the blood was starting to dry around a few large splinters of wood and several smaller ones. Her knees weakened, but she forced herself straight, determined to be strong.

"It's okay to lean on me," John said and increased his support at her waist. She was wan, her skin almost translucent, as the enormity of what had happened sank in.

She nodded and together they walked into the conference room, not that he felt safe now in any room with a glass wall. Except his house, since the prior owner— whom he had suspected had been involved in a less-than-legal venture—had installed bulletproof glass in all the windows.

He sat her down and Miles hurried into the room barely seconds later, a red first-aid box in his hand. Miles placed it on the table beside him. His gaze skipped across his brother's and there was no missing the worry there. That and a nervous tic along his jaw and his general jumpiness as he ripped his gaze away and started to pace by an inside wall of the room.

Mia glanced his way, watching his nervous back-and-forth, while John took out an alcohol pad.

"This may sting," he said.

Mia only nodded—all her attention was focused on Miles. She barely moved as he wiped away the dried blood. She flinched, her body doing a little jump, when he pulled out the biggest of the splinters. Blood immediately leaked from the small hole, and he dabbed at it, but then quickly yanked out the other splinters so he could clean the entire area and bandage it.

Luckily, he had just finished when Trey rushed into the room, but his eagle eyes immediately zeroed in on the bright white bandage on Mia's hand.

He hurried over, kneeled before his sister and took hold of her injured hand. "You're hurt."

"It's nothing really," she said weakly and braved a smile.

"When I get the bastard, he's going to be sorry," Trey said and brushed a hand across her cheek.

"How did he know where we were? We haven't been out of the building in well over a day," Mia said, then glanced in John's direction and then over at Miles.

John tracked her gaze to where Miles continued to pace like a caged tiger, back and forth, back and forth, in front of the inside wall of the room.

"Miles?" John said to draw his attention.

His brother stopped short and faced him but remained silent. His fists were clenched and that nervous tic jumped along his jaw.

"Did you notice anyone following you?" John asked.

Miles immediately shook his head in denial, but then seemed to reconsider. Tossing his hands up in the air, he said, "I don't know, okay. I don't know."

John wanted to shout at him. Ask him how he could be so careless, but bit back the angry words. It would only add even more tension to what he was already sensing between them. Tension that was palpable to everyone in the room.

"Did you notice anyone following you?" he asked

again, carefully tempering his tone in the hopes that Miles would reconsider his earlier statement.

Miles shrugged and shook his head. "I don't think so. I left the condo, drove here and parked down the street. I didn't see anything out of the ordinary."

"Have you seen any strangers around lately?" Trey asked as he straightened to stand behind Mia, his hand on her shoulder in support.

Miles jammed his hands on his hips, pursed his lips and then blurted out, "Besides the attacker I stopped yesterday?"

The hard line of Trey's jaw warned that he didn't appreciate the sarcasm. "Besides that intruder."

"Nothing. No one," Miles confirmed with some bite.

But despite his assertion, John was convinced that the shooter had to have some connection to Miles. As his gaze locked with Trey's and then drifted down to Mia's, it was obvious they felt the same way.

Trying to give his brother some rope, but not so he would hang himself, he said, "Even if Miles was followed, that would only lead them to the building and not to this floor."

Trey nodded. "You're right."

Rachel came to the door of the conference room at that moment. "There are some officers here to see you."

"Would you come with me, John? Miles, would you mind staying with Mia? She doesn't look like she's up to being interrogated right now," Trey said, and John didn't miss the silent communication between the two siblings.

Miles nodded and John followed Trey out of the conference room. Officers Puente and Johnson from the day before were in the lobby alongside two officers from the CSI unit.

"Officers. Thanks for getting here so quickly," Trey said and motioned to John. "I believe you know Mr. Wilson from yesterday's…incident. If at all possible—"

"We understand this requires…discretion," Officer Puente said with dip of her head and gazed at the other officers, who likewise acknowledged the request.

"The bullets came in through my office window. We didn't see anything because we were too busy trying not to get shot," John said and took the lead, directing the police to his office. At the door, he hung back, understanding the importance of not contaminating the scene.

The two beat cops stayed with him while Trey entered with the CSI officers.

But as he waited there for them to do their job, he wondered what was going on with Mia and Miles in the conference room.

Chapter Twelve

Miles sat across from her, his gaze focused on his hands, which were clasped before him tightly. He rested his elbows on his thighs and bounced them up and down.

Everything about him grated on her, but she held back from attack mode. It would be better to try and reach him in other ways, not to mention her head and hand were throbbing.

"Is there any aspirin there?" she said and lifted her chin in the direction of the first-aid kit.

"Let me check," he said, then fumbled as he tried to open the kit, but once he got it open, he searched through it and found a small packet of aspirin. He handed it to her and said, "I'll get you some water."

He hurried from the room and returned a few minutes later with a bottle of water.

"Thank you," she said as she tore open the packet, then tossed back the aspirin with some water.

"We're lucky no one was seriously injured," Miles said as he resumed his seat and his bouncing. "It seems to me this all started as soon as John got involved with your family," Miles challenged and glared at her.

Wow, talk about the pot calling the kettle black. She was not about to let him turn the tables on her, however.

"Seems to me there have been problems for a while. Someone leaking news. Possibly short-selling the stock," she replied and carefully watched for his reaction.

The bouncing stopped and he splayed his hands on his knees, locked his gaze on hers. He had hazel eyes, like John, but they lacked the warmth and caring of his half brother's eyes.

"I had nothing to do with that," he said, voice as chilly as a glacier, hands tight on his knees.

"I didn't say you did. Why would I think that? Especially since you were so brave to confront that intruder yesterday," she said, forcing an almost cajoling tone into her voice.

"I had to stop him. John is the only family I have left," Miles said, but he said it in a practiced tone, as if he'd rehearsed it over and over in order to sound convincing. Much like he had sounded yesterday when speaking to the police officers.

Only he didn't sound convincing. At least not to her.

"Family means everything to me, Miles. Make no mistake I will do whatever it takes to protect them and John."

What little color remained on his face drained, as his skin turned a sickly green.

She hated to be pleased at his discomfort, but was happy that he'd recognized that her words weren't only a promise. They were a threat. If he was involved with whatever was going on, he would pay for that.

Satisfied he'd gotten the message, she sat back to wait for Trey and John to return.

"You were very lucky, Mr. Wilson," one CSI officer said as he dug out a bullet from the side of the desk while Trey hovered nearby.

Mia's brother was in worried mode, arms across his muscled chest and his blue gaze focused on whatever the CSI officers were doing.

John watched from across the room as the cop held up what he assumed was the bullet.

Trey leaned forward to peer at it, gaze narrowed. "50 cal?"

"50 cal. Like I said, lucky. The glass slowed the bullet— a little—and the downward trajectory kept the bullets from ripping through the desk."

And into Mia, Miles and me, John thought and his heart stopped for a beat before pounding so hard the sound echoed in his ears.

"There's blood here," said the other CSI agent, a young blonde woman who seemed barely out of her twenties.

John motioned to his hand. "Mia had some wood splinters in her hand from the first bullet."

"She was lucky she didn't get hit directly," the officer said and swabbed the blood to preserve a sample for evidence.

Trey gestured to the bullet holes and cracks in the glass. "This pattern indicates it was a high-speed bullet, right? 50 cals are usually slower."

The CSI agent nodded, raised his camera and snapped several photos of the bullet holes and cracks in the glass before he motioned to them. "You're right that the faster the bullet, the more cracks. 50 cals are usually slower unless—"

"It's a 50 BMG," the female agent said.

Puzzled, John peered at Trey, who was clearly not happy with the officer's comment.

"50 BMG means this person is possibly a sniper with a pretty pricey gun," Trey said.

The female officer nodded. "Even a cheaper gun, like the Serbu or ArmaLite, will run you a few thousand."

"What doesn't make sense is why they would blindly shoot at this office. They can't see through the film," said the male CSI officer, who was still inspecting the window glass.

No, they couldn't, but maybe it didn't matter to whoever was shooting. Maybe they had been willing to take out everyone in the room. Including Miles, but was that only coincidence or an intentional attempt to tie up any loose ends?

"No, they can't," Trey admitted and glanced in his direction. "We should round up everyone and get them to safer locations until we can get a handle on this."

John nodded. "I'm going to send my people to work remotely."

Trey arched an eyebrow. "Including Miles?"

John shook his head. "I assume these officers will want to interview everyone who was in this room and afterward... I think we need to have a talk with him."

"I agree," Trey said and turned to the officers. "We're ready whenever you are for the interviews."

"Officer Johnson and I can handle that," Officer Puente said, and the other officers confirmed that was in order.

"We'll send the information on any evidence we gather here or in the other building to Detective Lopez," the female CSI officer advised.

"We'd appreciate that and if we dig up anything, we'll be sure to reciprocate," Trey said with a thankful nod.

As Trey walked toward the door, John turned and returned to the conference room, where Mia and Miles were waiting. Undeniable tension simmered between them, creating an uneasy feel in the room.

The strain didn't lessen once Trey and the police officers walked in. Trey went straight to his sister. "How's the hand?"

"Fine," Mia said, even though she was pale and cradling her hand gingerly, obviously in pain.

"Would you mind answering a few questions?" Officer Puente asked.

"Not at all," Miles said, almost too eagerly. He sat up in the chair straighter and faced the two cops.

Officer Puente began questioning Miles about his earlier movements, much like they had done barely an hour earlier, and the answers remained much the same.

"You went straight to Mr. Wilson's office when you arrived. You didn't stop for coffee or talk to anyone else?" Officer Johnson said.

Miles shook his head. "I said hello to the receptionist and then went straight to my brother's office."

"Is that what you normally do?" Johnson asked.

"Sometimes. Sometimes I go to my office first. Get a coffee. That kind of thing," Miles said and peered between him and the officer. "Tell them, John. It wasn't anything out of the ordinary."

Officer Johnson looked in his direction, seeking that confirmation.

"Miles sometimes comes right to my office. Sometimes he doesn't," John said, thinking that wasn't unusual. But the timing of it coupled with the shooting worried him.

"Where were you standing when the first shot occurred?" Puente asked, pen poised above her notepad to record his answer.

"John was at the bookcase, emptying boxes because we'd just moved. Supposedly because we'd be safer here," he said and glared at Mia and Trey. "How'd that work out?" he added in challenge.

Trey gritted his teeth, biting back a response, but nothing was holding Mia back.

"How is it that you were conveniently present at yesterday's attack and again this morning?"

"So were you, Mia. You *and* John. Whatever is going on has nothing to do with me," Miles argued, but there was a waver in his voice that worried John.

"Mia and I had been together for at least an hour," he said, avoiding any mention of breakfast and how that might be misinterpreted by the officers. "But the shooting started right after you came in," John challenged.

Miles shot to his feet and whirled to face him. Agitated, he tapped his chest with both his hands. "You're accusing me, your blood, instead of virtual strangers," he said and wildly flung an arm out in the direction of Mia and Trey.

John forced calm into his voice and posture. "I didn't mean to accuse you. You're my brother. But maybe someone was following you—"

"I already told you that I didn't see anyone following me," Miles said and lifted his hands in a pleading motion.

"But maybe you're being tracked," Trey said in a calm tone. *Deadly calm*, John thought.

Miles glared at the siblings, and for a second, John thought Miles might accuse them again, but then he said, "Fine. Search me. Here, let me help."

Miles reached into his pockets and tossed his wallet,

keys and phone onto the conference-room table. Then he ripped off his smartwatch and placed it there, too.

Puente gave her partner a go-ahead command and the male officer walked over to Miles. "Please place your hands on the wall and spread your legs."

Miles assumed the position and the officer patted him down.

"Nothing here, Puente," he said.

The female cop motioned to the phone and watch. "CSI will want to take those for analysis."

A knock on the doorjamb drew their attention to where the CSI officers stood holding a knapsack.

Miles's knapsack, John realized, and a sick feeling oozed through his gut like an oil slick on water.

"Does this knapsack belong to one of you?" the female officer asked.

MIA'S HAND THROBBED PAINFULLY, but it was nothing compared to the pain visible on the faces of the two brothers. She felt for them, even Miles, as much as she distrusted him.

"It's my bag," Miles said, his voice barely above a whisper.

Mia glanced at the officer's badge and asked, "Is something wrong, Officer Maxwell?"

The young woman walked to the table, laid the knapsack on it and reached into one of the small side pockets. She removed something and placed it beside Miles's belongings. It was a small black-and-silver disk, just slightly larger than a quarter.

"An AirTag?" she whispered in surprise.

"That's not mine," Miles immediately said, shock obvious on his features.

"It's small enough and light enough to slip in without anyone noticing," John said, offering his brother an out.

Way too easy to do, Mia thought. "Aren't there safeguards—"

"He's using an Android phone and watch. They won't pick up that he's being tracked. If the service provider sees anything funky going on, they'll disable it," John explained.

"But not for a couple of days, right?" Trey asked.

"Three, I believe," John said.

"That means we have three days to use it to find whoever planted it," Mia said.

Chapter Thirteen

Her brother had had to pull in all kinds of favors for the CSI officers to leave the tracker with the SBS so they could attempt to draw out whoever had slipped it into Miles's knapsack.

If it had even been someone else, Mia thought, gazing at Miles as he sat in one of the interior conference rooms they had on their floor. For safety's sake, SBS had sent everyone with glass-walled offices to work at home.

"Did anyone else have access to your knapsack?" Trey asked as he angrily paced back and forth across the room.

Miles pursed his lips and shrugged. "Just me as far as I know."

As much as she didn't want to give him another out, Mia said, "Anyone get too close or bump you in the last day or so?"

He shook his head. "Not that I can recall."

Trey nodded and looked at his cousins. "Can you do anything with the tracker?"

"We can get the serial number and contact the authorities to try to get the provider to reveal the identity of the person who owns the account," Sophie advised.

With a sarcastic smile, Robbie added, "Good luck with that but maybe there are other things we can do."

"Like what?" Mia asked.

"Like things you might not want to know," Sophie admitted with a half smile and laugh.

Mia held her hands up in a don't-tell-me gesture. "What about drawing them out?" she asked.

"And risk having someone shot or worse?" her father challenged from across the width of the table and peered at the white bandage on her hand.

"I'm fine," she said even though her hand still throbbed.

"Mia's right, *Papi*. We can't just sit here and wait for another attack," Trey said as he stood beside her and rested his hands on the top of the leather chair.

THE TWO SIBLINGS *were determined*, John thought, but like their father, Ramon, he was worried about another possible attack.

"I don't want to risk anyone's life," he said.

"Too late. This person is already after the family and now, after you and Miles. I'm sure your program would tell you that if you ran the data," Mia challenged, her dimpled chin tilted up defiantly.

"She knows about the program?" Miles said, accusation ringing in his tone. He looked all around the table and his eyebrows raised as the truth of the situation sank in. "They all know. You told them all about the 'top-secret' program," he said, emphasizing the words with bunny-ear fingers.

"It was necessary, Miles," he defended.

Miles laughed with derision. "Yeah. Sure."

Trey's smartphone rang, saving John from having to say anything else to ease his brother's wounded pride.

"Mi amor," Trey said and turned his back on the

room as he walked to the farthest wall to listen to Roni, he guessed.

Trey murmured his agreement at whatever his fiancée reported. "I get it. Thank him for the info. Please copy Sophie and Robbie when you send the video. See you later and watch your six. We've got a psychopath here."

A psychopath. Not an understatement, John thought and his gaze was drawn to Mia's hand again. His heart constricted with the thought that he might have lost her earlier that day. If she had been standing just a few inches over, the bullet would have struck her.

Trey returned to the table. "Roni has a list of recently released gang members for our review. They weren't able to get any prints or casings from the rooftop, but the chopper got some video of the shooter. So did the building's CCTV cameras. Like he did at your old location, he got in through the service area."

"It's someone who's familiar with those areas," Mia offered.

"Contractors. Inspectors. Delivery people. Garbagemen. Mail persons," John said, thinking of all the possible workers who would have regular access to those areas.

"We can cross-reference that list of gang members with current employment to see if anything clicks," Sophie said.

"If you can send me the videos, I'll run it against the earlier ones to see if the physical characteristics are the same," John said.

"Mia and I can review the list the old-fashioned way and see what we can come up with," Trey said and laid a hand on Mia's shoulder.

Miles did a quick toss of his hands. "And what do I sit here and do?"

An uncomfortable silence filled the room.

John sucked in a deep breath, then released it and said in a rush of words, "It's not that we don't trust you, Miles."

"But you don't, John. I've had those vibes from you for months, ever since…the leak," Miles said and looked away from him, which only heightened John's unease.

"That leak really hurt the company, but benefitted someone, Miles. Was it you?"

Miles continued to look away, but then with a resigned shrug and shake of his head, he said, "You don't understand, John."

Mia rose and said, "Maybe Miles and John need some privacy."

Sophie and Robbie snapped their laptops closed, stood and followed Ramon, Trey and Mia out of the room. But as she walked by, Mia offered John a supportive smile and pass of her injured hand across his arm.

He offered her a strained smile and once they were gone, he closed the door and leaned against it. Staring hard at his brother, he said, "What is it that I don't understand, Miles?"

Shaking his head, Miles shot to his feet and paced, still avoiding his gaze. "It's not easy being your brother."

"And that's the reason you leaked the info? Sold our stock short? *Our* company stock, Miles," he said, almost shouting the words.

"*Your* company," Miles shouted back. "*Your* company, *your* ideas. Me, I'm just along for the ride," Miles said and pounded his chest in frustration.

John shook his head and tempered his anger, seeing Miles's pain. "That's not true. You're an important part—"

Miles slashed his hand to silence him. "Would you have hired me if I wasn't your brother?"

He couldn't immediately answer, in part because the truth would be too painful. But if there was a time to cause pain in the hopes of fixing whatever had gone wrong in their relationship, it was now.

"You didn't have the qualifications for the job, but I knew you could do it," he confessed.

Miles dragged a hand through his hair in frustration and finally faced him. "But I haven't, have I? I'm nothing more than a glorified administrative assistant because you don't trust me with anything valuable."

"This software is too important to share," he said, but Miles raised his eyebrows and held his hands wide.

"Everyone who just left this room knows about it. I'd bet that the two tech dweebs even have access to it. Am I wrong?"

"They do know, but, no, they don't have access to it. But I would trust them with it," John said.

Miles thumped his chest once again with his fingers. "But not your flesh and blood."

"Are you responsible for the leak? Did you sell the stock short?" John pressed, needing to know.

Miles's shoulders slumped and he looked away as he said, "I did."

John's chest hurt so much he almost couldn't breathe. Throat constricted with emotion, he drew in an anguished breath and was barely able get out the single word. "Why?"

With a little shrug, Miles said, "I wanted to be rich enough that I wouldn't have to rely on your charity."

"Charity? It's not charity—you're my brother," he said and walked toward Miles, but his brother held up a hand to stop him.

"Half brother," Miles reminded him.

John couldn't believe what he was hearing. "I've never thought of you that way."

"But that's what I am and a bastard son at that. Your father reminded me of it often enough," Miles said, the tone of his voice slipping from his earlier antagonism into a well of darkness and pain.

"My father... He was an evil man. You kept us safe from him," John said, then walked over and embraced his brother.

Miles remained stiff in John's arms at first, then shook him off and took a step away.

"I brought this danger to your doorstep," Miles said softly.

"You know who he is?" John said, saddened that what he and the others had suspected all along was proving true.

Miles shook his head. "Not really. I didn't get a name."

"But you saw him?" John pressed.

Miles did another small shake of his head. "No. I asked around and he called me. Asked me what I wanted. Told me what it would cost and where to leave the money."

And he'd obviously done just that. "What was he supposed to do?"

With a stiff jerk of his head, he said, "Come into the office and act scary. Run off when I confronted him."

"Nothing else?" John asked.

"Nothing else," Miles admitted.

"And you did this to scare me?" John asked, needing to have the entire story.

"Sometimes when you looked at me lately, I could tell you didn't trust me. I figured that if I was a hero all of a sudden, you might think differently," Miles confessed with a little shrug.

Because if he thought differently, John might trust him enough to give him access to his new project. "You already were a hero to me, Miles," he said sadly, then walked to the door of the conference room and opened it.

He didn't need to say anything else. Couldn't do anything else as Miles walked to the door and paused. "You know where to send my stuff," his brother said and hurried down the hall toward the reception area.

John watched him turn the corner to go to the elevators and he wondered if that was going to be the last time he ever saw his brother.

He was standing there when Mia stepped into the hall and looked down his way, worry etched on her beautiful features.

What he wanted most was to crawl into a hole somewhere and hide, but he couldn't. Straightening his spine, he walked toward her. The Gonzalez family needed him right now. Mia needed him and he wasn't about to fail her.

As he neared, she held out her uninjured hand and he slipped his hand into hers.

"Are you okay?" she said and tucked herself into his side, offering comfort.

I will be as long as you're here, he thought, but kept it to himself. It was too new and complicated between them.

"I have something to tell you," he said and recounted what Miles had said, but kept some things to himself, still unable to share everything because he was processing it himself.

She accepted that was all he was willing to share at that moment. That intuition was probably what made her so good at dealing with the people she met at her various social events and he was grateful that she didn't press for more when he finished.

JOHN WORE THE hurt of his brother's betrayal the way a priest of old might wear a hair shirt, with grace and elegance even though it was causing great discomfort.

Mia raked her fingers through a lock of his hair that had fallen forward, leaned close and whispered, "I'm here if you need me."

He smiled, but it didn't reach his hazel eyes, which were flat and a darker brown with his upset.

He said nothing and she didn't press.

She walked him into the unused office they had grabbed to leave him and Miles alone in the conference room. It belonged to a marketing manager who was on maternity leave and wouldn't be back for several months.

Sophie and Robbie were at a small table at one end while Trey sat at the desk, reviewing the list Roni had sent over. Mia had been working with him, going over the police files in search of anyone who might have the telltale tattoo, or had access to buildings in the downtown area.

She gestured to the desk and said, "Trey and I have a number of possible suspects, but we still have quite a few to review."

"Too many," Trey said, exasperation in his voice.

"Why don't you send me the list to run through the program?" John said.

"Aren't you going to do the videos?" she asked and shook her head as she realized. "A supercomputer. I bet it can do multiple things at once."

"Like you can if you want to keep me from getting hangry," Trey teased.

"Sexist much?" she teased right back.

"Not sexist at all," Robbie said. "You know all the best places to eat in the area. If you left it up to us it would be the same old, same old."

"Good save, Rob," Sophie said with a laugh.

A save, but true, she had to admit. "I'll order food and set it up in the conference room again. Is *Papi* still around? Should I order for him?"

Trey shook his head. "He's gone home to deal with *Mami* before it hits the news."

Mia understood. Mama Bear Samantha would go into full protective mode once she'd heard, but they needed her to stay out of it and safe at home. She didn't ask about Miles since he'd bolted after his talk with John.

"I'll go order," she said and hurried from the room to call a local Thai restaurant. A warm meal would keep them because she suspected that it might take some time to get any results, analyze them and decide on a course of action.

She selected a variety of items and, using the alias they'd created for deliveries to the SBS, she placed the order. The security guard downstairs would make the payment on their behalf from a cash drawer and send another guard up with the food. It was how they kept confidentiality when dealing with certain clients, and in this case, maybe kept their killer from tampering with their food.

While she waited for the delivery, she set out plates, napkins, cups and soda, and also took a moment to grab some aspirin to dull the ache in her hand. As much as it hurt, it chilled her to think that it could have been much worse.

"How are you doing?" John asked as he walked into the room and set his laptop on the table. Assorted lines and numbers flashed across the screen as the programs continued to run.

"I should be asking you that," she said and wrapped her arms around him when he approached.

"I'll…survive," he said, and she didn't press for more. There would be time enough for that after their late lunch.

They stood there, wrapped together in the comfort of the embrace until Mia's phone rang to warn the delivery had arrived.

"I have to get that," she said.

"Let me help," he said but she shook her head.

"Better no one sees you're up here," she warned and raced off without him.

Julia had accepted the delivery and helped her carry the bags to the conference room. "Do you need help setting it up?" the young Latina asked as she placed the bag on a credenza.

"I can help," John said and waved off her assistance.

"Don't let me keep you from work," Mia said, and John smirked. Again.

"Supercomputer. I get it. Too bad it has us all getting killed soon," she joked, then removed the take-out dishes from the bags and placed them on the credenza.

John did the same and soon the enticing smells of lemongrass, various chilies, garlic and ginger wafted into the air.

Almost on cue, Trey strolled into the room along with Sophie and Robbie. Her cousins placed their laptops on the table and walked over to look at the various dishes Mia had ordered.

"Looks good, Mia," Robbie said and grabbed a plate.

"It's one of my favorite places. You've got pad Thai, *som tam,* which is a green papaya salad, fried rice, stir-fried water spinach and that omelet is called *kai jeow.* I didn't forget about your sweet tooth, Trey. That roti has bananas and condensed milk."

"You're the best, Mia," Trey said and playfully hugged her.

She waited off to one side as Trey, Robbie and Sophie prepared plates for themselves.

John stood beside her, waiting for her to take some food. "After you," he said and she smiled in thanks, grabbed a plate and served herself some pad Thai, spinach and a slice of the *kai jeow.*

John followed suit but grabbed a second plate, where he loaded a couple of pieces of the roti.

"I guess Trey isn't the only one with a sweet tooth," Mia teased.

JOHN WANTED TO say that he was sweet on her, but knew she wouldn't appreciate it in front of her family. He'd keep it for what he hoped would be another kissing session that night. Maybe even more, but not in the penthouse suite, he realized. That was no longer a secure area.

Once he was sitting at the table, Mia beside him, he shot her a quick look before he said, "I was thinking that since Mia and I seem to be his primary targets right now, it would make sense for us to move somewhere safer tonight."

Trey narrowed his gaze and a puzzled look slipped over Mia's features.

"Your place in Indian Creek? The one on the water with all the glass?" Trey asked as he forked up some rice.

John held his hands up, asking for a chance to explain. "You've had your guards there for over a day. It is on the water, but all the window glass is bulletproof."

"Bulletproof?" Mia said, her doubt obvious.

With a sheepish shrug, he said, "I don't know what the prior owner did, but he valued his safety."

"Drug lord," Robbie said with a fake cough and earned the now almost familiar elbow from his sister. The shot was so hard, it shook loose a piece of green papaya on Robbie's fork.

"Maybe, but lucky for us since John's right that they can't stay in the penthouse tonight," Trey said.

"Do I have any say in this?" Mia asked and forked up some of the egg dish.

"Of course, but do you have any better suggestions?" John pressed, pausing with a forkful of spinach half-way to his mouth.

"I don't, but I'd like some say in what to do," she said and relented. "It makes sense to go there. We won't be safe here or at the penthouse at the Del Sol."

"What about your brother? Seems to me someone was taking a shot at him as well," Trey said and finished the last of the food on his plate.

Peering at the tabletop, he ran an index finger across the wood grain in an uneasy gesture, but then forged ahead, revealing the explosive information he'd kept to himself earlier. "Miles is…out of the picture."

Mia shook her head, her gaze shuttered as she said, "What does that mean?"

"He confessed he was responsible for the leak so he could short the stock. He also admitted to hiring the goon who attacked us yesterday," he said, feeling not only the anger and pain again, but also stupid that he hadn't listened to what his gut had told him.

Mia reached out and took hold of his hand, drawing his gaze to her. He had expected to see pity there, but instead he saw righteous anger on his behalf. Armed with that, he said, "He told me he didn't see who he hired. He made the arrangements over the phone and was told where to leave the payment."

"This gun-for-hire may have been following Miles even if he hadn't realized it. He probably slipped the tracker in his bag," Mia said and gave his hand a reassuring squeeze.

"Maybe when we have our list of suspects, we can get Miles to come back and look at the photos to see if any of them look familiar. Maybe he saw the attacker and didn't realize it," Trey suggested and stood to get more food.

Considering how it had ended with Miles, John wasn't sure his brother would be cooperative, but he didn't say. Instead, he returned his attention to the meal, even though the food was tasteless from his upset. The others around the table weren't as fazed, and seemed to be enjoying the meal Mia had selected.

"Don't like it?" Mia asked.

"It's very good, I'm just not really hungry," he lied and was spared from continuing the conversation when his laptop pinged to warn that one of the operations had finished.

He examined the results and smiled.

Chapter Fourteen

"The program finished the analysis on the videos from the chopper and CCTV. There's a 95-percent probability it's the same person from the drive-bys and the attack in our office," John said and swiveled his laptop around so the others could see.

Mia stared hard at the results, heart pounding. There was no doubting any longer that whoever was after her family had managed to weave himself into the lives of John's family, and despite her anger at Miles, she worried about his safety.

"We're together, but Miles doesn't have any protection," she said.

"He doesn't and whether Miles knows it or not, he may be able to lead us to this killer," Sophie said and picked up the tracker that had been sitting in the middle of the table.

"I don't think the killer would be stupid enough to let us find him via his cloud account," Mia said, puzzled by what her cousin was suggesting.

"That's true, but if he's actively tracking, his phone is accessing that cloud account regularly," Sophie said.

Robbie immediately jumped into the discussion. "But

the location of the tracker is being sent using Crowd GPS and those transmissions are encrypted."

"Crowd GPS?" Mia asked, not as familiar as her cousins or John about how the tracker worked.

John picked up his phone as he explained. "The tracker connects to your phone using your Bluetooth, and when it does, it sends the location to the cloud account."

"Wouldn't someone notice that the tracker was connecting to their phone?" she asked.

"The connection is very quick and uses little data so unless you set up your phone to warn you or use some kind of scanner or app on an Android phone, you wouldn't know," John advised and set his phone back on the tabletop.

"And the data being sent is encrypted, which makes things a little harder, but not impossible," Robbie said.

"If I'm hearing you right, you want to try and monitor where those signals are being sent to find the cloud account?" Trey said, finally piping up from where he had been sitting silently, finishing his meal, but clearly following the discussion.

Sophie and Robbie nodded in unison. "We do," Sophie said.

"Miles said he got a call from the killer. Maybe he has a phone number," Mia offered.

"It's likely a burner phone," Trey countered.

John immediately responded, obviously onboard with her and her cousins. "But it could be a burner app on the phone he's using to access the cloud account. If it is, he's leaving digital information all over the place. If we reach out to the phone provider—"

"We'll get information on the cell towers and other

things, which may give us his location or a connection to our list of suspects," Trey said, finishing for him.

"Will Miles help us?" Mia asked, realizing that John's half brother's cooperation might help them move a step closer to catching the killer.

John splayed his hands on the table, hesitating, but then with a heavy sigh, he said, "I hope he will."

JOHN DROVE THE nondescript black BMW that Trey had offered him from SBS's pool of vehicles. Mia was in the car beside him, and he hoped that with her people skills she might be a help in what was likely to be another painful discussion with his brother. As observant as she was, he also hoped she'd be able to pick up on anything unusual going on in the area.

It didn't take long for them to go from downtown Miami to his brother's South Pointe condo. The tall building was within walking distance to South Beach and adjacent to South Pointe Park and Biscayne Bay.

John pulled into the underground garage and parked. He hesitated because he wasn't sure of what kind of reception he would get, or how he would respond, for that matter. His gut churned with anger and pain every time he thought about what his brother, his only family, had done to him.

Mia's reassuring touch came on his hand. "It's going to be okay."

He met her gaze and plastered a tight smile on his face. "I used to tell myself that as a kid when my dad…" His throat choked up and he couldn't continue.

Mia brushed the back of her hand across his cheek, leaned across the narrow distance in the car and whispered a kiss across his lips. "You have us now, too."

He nodded. "Thank you. I guess we should go."

With a dip of her head, she exited the car and reached into the back seat to grab Miles's knapsack with the tracker tucked back into the side pocket, just like the killer had left it.

He got out of the car and grabbed his own knapsack. As he did so, he noticed an SBS guard off to one side of the garage. From his position, the guard would have a view of anyone entering through the garage entrance or going to the elevator and stairs into the building. Trey had clearly arranged for protection and he was grateful for that.

Placing a hand at the small of Mia's back, he applied gentle pressure to guide her in the direction of the building entrance and once they were in the lobby, he waved at the building security guards who let them access the elevators to Miles's condo. With each floor they climbed, John's tension increased until he was almost bouncing on his feet in anticipation. Much like she had done before, Mia slipped her hand into his and with that comfort, some of his apprehension eased.

He wasn't surprised when Miles yanked open his door even before they reached it.

He stood there, arms across his chest, his face as hard and cold as a death mask.

"I didn't expect to see you so soon," Miles said, voice flat and chilly.

"May we come in, Miles?" Mia said in a stern voice.

He almost sneered at her, but stepped aside to let them enter.

When John walked into the condo, it was dark, since every window shade and blind had been pulled low to block any view into the rooms. Normally there would be a vast expanse of Fisher Island, Miami and Biscayne Bay visible from the panoramic windows.

In his mind's eye, he recalled what other buildings were nearby and could understand his brother's fear. There was another tall tower to the north and quite a number of tall residential buildings on Fisher Island across the way although only homeowners could access that private island.

"What do you want?" Miles said as he followed them into his living room, but hung back, away from the windows.

Mia held his knapsack out to him, but Miles hesitated, eyeing it dubiously. To his surprise, Mia said, "Yes, the tracker is in there. We need your help."

Miles almost recoiled, but then shook his head and laughed. "Gotta give it to you, Mia. You've got brass. Not sure what I can do," he said, then grabbed the knapsack from her and tossed it on the granite breakfast bar.

John motioned to the knapsack. "The tracker will probably stay active for a couple of days. We want you to hold on to it for now."

"So I can be a sitting duck?" Miles said with a haughty lift of a sandy-colored eyebrow.

"My brother has arranged for extra security around the condo, and he's talked to building security as well," Mia explained.

There was a visible release of the tension in his brother's body until he gestured to the windows.

"Not much we can do there, Miles. But I ran the probability of the killer—"

"Killer?" he said in surprise.

Mia nodded. "We think the man you hired accepted

the job to get closer to my family and we think he already murdered Jorge Hernandez."

Miles traced his finger through the air, as if connecting the dots. "Wasn't that the developer who blew up his own building and killed himself?"

"One and the same," John confirmed.

Miles shook his head roughly and blew out a harsh breath. "I really messed up bad. I'm so, so sorry, John."

For too long he'd accepted his brother's various excuses for the things he did carelessly, but maybe it was time for some tough love. "*Sorry* isn't going to cut it this time, Miles. Like Mia said, we need your help."

He detected something in Miles's gaze as he narrowed it to peer at him. Admiration maybe. When Miles nodded, he said, "What do you need me to do?"

"Hold on to the knapsack and act like you didn't find it. Stay home," John instructed.

"You mentioned that you spoke to the killer on the phone. Do you have his number?" Mia asked.

"He hid his number when he called," Miles said. He reached into his back pocket, pulled out the phone the CSI team had returned and handed it to John. "You know the security code."

He accepted the phone and unlocked it to scroll through the calls. "The number's hidden, but we may still be able to trace the origin of the call."

"Did you notice anything about the caller's voice? An accent or anything?" Mia asked.

With a shrug, he said, "He sounded kind of like you."

Eyes wide with surprise, Mia said, "Like me?"

Miles nodded. "Yes, like you and some of the other Cubans I've met in Miami. It's just…something. An accent, I guess."

"It's a start, I guess. It could mean he's a Cuban-American," John said.

"You never saw him, but he had to get close enough to slip that tracker in your bag. We're working on a list of suspects. Would you mind taking a look to see if any of them look familiar?" Mia asked, taking the lead on the discussion.

"I'll do whatever you need me to do. I never meant for any of this to happen. You've got to believe that, John," Miles pleaded.

"I do believe it, but actions have consequences," he said, not wanting his brother to think that he could wheedle his way out of this problem.

Miles nodded. "I get it. There's no get-out-of-jail-free card this time."

"No, there isn't," he responded.

To his relief, Mia stepped in to ease the growing discomfort. "Thank you for your help, Miles. Know that we are doing what we can to keep you safe. We'll let you know when we need you to do anything else."

"Whatever you need," he said and walked them back to the door.

Mia exited and John followed, but he stopped to face his brother. "Thank you, Miles."

His brother's grim smile confirmed that he understood. It was a thank-you for the past and possibly a goodbye as well.

That Mia had sensed the undercurrents as well became clear as she wrapped her arms around him in the elevator and held him tight, silently offering comfort.

They rode the elevator down to the parking structure, but before they exited, John peered out to confirm the security guard was still there.

He escorted Mia to the car for the drive to his home, anxious about what she would think of it when she saw it. Unlike the Lamborghini and the Del Sol penthouse that Miles had favored to make a statement, he had chosen the Indian Creek home because it had appealed to him with its stunning views of Biscayne Bay and all of Miami to the south.

He'd actually bought the place for just the location, since he'd gutted most of the interior, which had been a style he might have described as Versailles meets Broadway. He'd wanted a calmer, more natural vibe to have a retreat away from his high-tech world. He hoped she'd see that and appreciate it.

"You said you live in Indian Creek?" she asked, breaking the initial silence in the car as he drove up A1A in the direction of the exclusive community.

"I bought the place just after I sold my start-up," he said while keeping a close eye on traffic and the rear-view mirror to make sure they weren't being followed. As he did so, he realized that Mia had pulled down her visor even though it was dusk. She was also diligently watching his six.

"Did you really buy it from a drug lord?" she said with a laugh, recalling Robbie's comment.

"If he was, he didn't admit it. The closing was done electronically so I never got to meet him," he said, imagining what the owner of the home with the over-the-top decor might look like.

Mia read his thoughts. "I imagine that he might have been…unique."

"Tactful, very tactful. The house took a lot of work," he said, but he didn't get a chance to explain as Mia's phone rang through the car's speakers.

She waved the phone in the air so he could see it. "It's Trey," she said and when she answered, his voice filled the interior of the BMW.

"How did it go?" Trey asked.

"Miles is going to cooperate. Unfortunately, the killer hid their phone number, but I'm assuming we can still use Miles's phone number to try and track things," Mia said.

"Roni is asking the provider to give us the call detail records. I'm almost done making my list of possible suspects from the report Roni sent over. I should have it by the time you get to John's," Trey advised.

In the background Roni called out, "I've flagged my favorites on the list."

"My program's analysis is done as well, but I haven't had a chance to review it. Once I do, I will send it along," John said as he stopped at a light near North Beach Oceanside Park.

"Sounds good. Roni and I are investigating a few other leads and if we have anything new, we'll call. Hopefully Sophie and Robbie will have something soon as well," Trey said and hung up.

There was a moment of silence again as they waited for the light to turn green, but when they were moving again, Mia said, "Do you think my cousins will be able to get anything on that cloud account?"

John sighed and shook his head. "That's tough to say. It's probably going to be almost impossible to hack into the user's cloud account to get any info. I'm sure the company has major defenses."

MIA HAD WORRIED about that as well, but if anyone could get in it would be Sophie and Robbie. They had inherited their NSA parents' computer smarts and she trusted not only their abilities, but also their ethics. As people who used their hacking skills, understanding the balance between what they could do and what they should do made all the difference in the world. Which reminded her of the conversation she'd had with John just the night before about the Manhattan Project and his concerns about how his program could be abused. But she kept silent about that since there were so many other worries to think about.

In no time, John was turning onto 91st Street to cross over to Indian Creek Island Road. By now dusk had completely fallen, and only the faintest rays of sunlight crept above the horizon while the deeper blues and purples of night colored the darkening sky. There were no streetlights along the road, just the lights coming on in homes set close to the water. In the areas surrounding Indian Creek and to the south, lights flickered on like fireflies on a summer night.

John continued until he was almost at the dead-center point of the island and then turned into a driveway. As he did, she caught sight of the SBS security guard sitting in a car parked near the mouth of the driveway, nose pointed toward the road in case he had to move quickly.

When John parked in front of his home, there was another car with a security guard in a ready position. As they got out, Mia grabbed the overnight bag Roni had packed for her that morning from the back seat. When they approached the door, the guard stepped out of the car, and John positioned himself in front of her in a protective gesture, his body tense.

"Mr. Wilson. Ms. Gonzalez. Ted Masters," he said and pulled out an SBS photo ID.

John relaxed, stepped aside and shook the man's hand. "Mr. Masters. Nice to meet you."

Mia greeted the man as well, recognizing him as one of Trey's older, former colleagues. "You used to be with Miami PD."

He acknowledged it with a dip of his head and a warm smile. "I was. Trey made me an offer I couldn't refuse."

"Thank you for being here," Mia said, appreciating that he was there to protect them.

With a wave of his hand toward the house, Masters said, "We have another man in the back and the guard at the gate and me will take turns checking the grounds. We have replacements coming in the morning."

"We appreciate anything you can do, Mr. Masters," John said and with another handshake, they left the guard and walked into the house.

When they entered, John stepped away from her, a sheepish look on his face.

"Welcome to my home," he said.

Chapter Fifteen

John held his breath, waiting for her reaction as she sauntered into the open-concept space that held his living and dining areas and a large gourmet kitchen. The lights he'd programmed had come on automatically, casting warm light at various spots throughout the room.

She almost twirled around like a ballerina as she took in his home, and when she faced him, her smile was brilliant.

"This is lovely. It's so…peaceful," she said.

It pleased him that she had gotten the vibe he had been hoping to create. He walked toward her and slipped his hand into hers when she held it out to him.

"I wanted it to be…zen is what the designer called it," he admitted, and also looked around his home as if seeing it for the first time.

Mia shook her head. "This is all you, not just the designer's."

The heat of a blush swept up his face. "I think she got a little frustrated with me at times, but this was going to be my home." A home that he had thought about sharing with her more than once even though they'd only dated a few times. She'd made that kind of impression on him and in the two days that had passed, she'd only cemented her place in his heart.

"Thanks. Let me show you to your bedroom so you can get comfortable," he said, and with gentle pressure on the small of her back, he led her to a bedroom that was on the opposite side from his wing in the house.

She strolled slowly, taking in his home the way a foodie sampled a fine meal. She paused to examine a painting and side table tucked into a small niche in the hall. A wrought-iron candlestick and fragrant eucalyptus candle sat on the table beside a palm-leaf-shaped tray holding an assortment of local shells and rustic balls made with twigs and rattan.

"It's a beautiful landscape," she said and then leaned forward to peer more carefully at the artist's signature. "Wilson? Any relation?"

He smiled. "My mom. She used to paint."

"She's a wonderful artist," she said, then asked, "Is that where you used to live?"

"Determined, aren't you?" he teased because of her continued attempts to find out more about his past.

She held her hands up in a why-not gesture and gave him a flirty grin. "It would be easier if you just told me."

It would be easier, but not as much fun. "Maybe later after we get some work done."

That seemed to satisfy her for the moment since she did that little ballerina whirl again and walked down the hall to the two guest bedrooms.

"You can have either, but I'd suggest the room to the right. It has great views of the water," he said, gesturing toward the room.

"Thanks. I'll only be a few minutes while I unpack. Where should I meet you?" she said.

"Take your time. I have an office in the other wing, but I like working at the dining-room table," he said. While he'd built the office to have everything he could need and to be comfortable, he preferred the wide-open spaces and views from the dining room.

"I'll meet you there," she said, and he left her to also slip into his usual at-home sweats and T-shirt. Better she see the real him and not whatever ideas she'd gotten from the various articles about him or their encounters at the Del Sol parties. He had hoped that he'd let her see that real him on their few dates, but then she'd suddenly stopped seeing him. *Maybe she hadn't liked the real you*, he wondered as he hurriedly changed and returned to the dining room to set up his laptop and print out his program's analysis of the possible suspects along with the report that Trey had sent.

In the distance came the whir of the printer in his office as it spat out the pages. He went to pick up the papers, and as he did so, the opening and closing of cabinets in his kitchen caught his attention. After the last page came out, he grabbed them and returned to the dining-room table.

Mia was in the kitchen, searching through cabinets. She faced him and said, "Not snooping. Just trying to find the fixings for some coffee."

"Not a problem," he said, then walked over and pointed out where everything was in the kitchen. *"Mi casa, su casa."*

"Gracias, mi amor," she said with a teasing light in her blue gaze, but the words still made his privates tighten as he imagined her saying it while they made love.

He rushed away, then immediately sat to hide his very obvious reaction and busied himself with placing the two reports side by side so they could compare them. As he began his review, the whir of the burr grinder intruded as she milled the beans. He looked over to watch her. Appreciate the sight of her in leggings that hugged luscious Cuban curves. The soft fabric of her T-shirt was tight against her generous breasts, but looser around her middle.

He dragged his gaze away from her to quell his desire and buried his head in the report.

Scant minutes later, the earthy aroma of coffee wafted over. Just the smell alone was enough to lift some of the tiredness he was feeling from the very taxing and emotional day. After all, how often was it that a sniper tried to take you out and you found out your brother had betrayed you?

He'd been so distracted by those thoughts and her presence, he realized he hadn't processed anything on the page he'd just finished reading.

Flipping back to the first page of his program's analysis, he was about to start again when Mia came over with mugs of coffee. She placed his in front of him, and he took a sip. It was perfect.

"Thanks. I need a boost of energy," he said and set down the mug, away from the papers.

"You'll get it with that much sugar and caffeine," she said and cradled the mug in both hands as she sipped her coffee.

"Can I help?" she asked.

"Sure," he said and laid the report on the table between them. They went through the report together line by line, only stopping so he could run into his office for paper and pens to take notes.

By the time they'd finished, they had made a list of

the highest probability suspects identified by his program and it was an eclectic mix from young one-time minor offenders to hardened felons.

"Do you know why the program chose these men?" Mia asked as she looked at her list and did another flip through the pages of the report.

"I wish I did, but there are so many paths in the neural network I programmed that it's hard to say why it made those decisions," he confessed.

HIS WORDS REMINDED Mia again about some of the materials she'd read when she was trying to find out more about John and what he did for a living. It was when she'd seen the article about programs that identified schizophrenia. She'd learned more about what he did, but not who he was, which she'd found frustrating because he intrigued her. Even more so with all that had happened in the weeks since she'd first met him.

"This is what Trey and Roni came up with," he said and placed that report on the table between them. As they had before, they carefully examined each of the suspects and the notes that Trey and Roni had made for each one. They had apparently focused not only on the past crimes of the suspects, but also on things like whether they had tattoos, jobs in downtown buildings, or relatives who had also been in trouble with the law.

"They did a lot of work in a short time," Mia said.

"And there's quite a few points that overlap," John said as he laid out his pad with his notes and gestured to several suspects that had made it to both of their lists.

"That's amazing," she said, impressed by what her brother and his fiancée had assembled in just a couple of hours and how it had produced results similar to those from John's program.

"Looks like Trey and Roni's police guts are as good as your computer," she said.

"Reminds me of that Hepburn-Tracy movie where the librarian outsmarts the computer," John admitted.

"*Desk Set*," Mia said.

"Huh?" he said, puzzled.

"That's the name of the movie. *Desk Set*. I love those old black-and-whites," she admitted.

He smiled and said, "So do I. I've got a collection of them if you want to watch one later."

She grinned, happy to find out that one little tidbit about him. "I'd like that."

"Let's make a list of these suspects and add my computer's probabilities for each one," he said.

They got to work on the final list, identifying the most likely candidates to discuss with Trey and Roni. When they were done, John scanned the list with his phone and sent it to Trey with a request that they call when they were ready.

While they waited, Mia refreshed their coffees and he pulled out some menus from the kitchen junk drawer so they could think about dinner before it got too late.

She had barely laid out the menus on the table when Trey video-called them. He cast the call to his laptop and motioned for Mia to join him.

"Looks like we all agree on a number of people," Trey said and held up a copy of the list.

"We do, but that's assuming the information we started with was reliable," John cautioned.

"Garbage in, garbage out," Mia chimed in, but she

quickly added, "But I trust what Roni did to produce this list."

"If our basic premise was right, namely, that he was a gang member," Roni cautioned, and the earlier optimism Mia had felt dimmed with Roni's warning.

John must have sensed it since he reached out to offer comfort, covering her hand with his. "We have to start somewhere, Mia. It's a good start and if it isn't... we'll start again."

Roni nodded. "It's a solid start. I'd bet my badge on it. But if we're going to be able to charge whoever it is, we're going to have to follow the official route."

"Meaning?" Mia asked.

"An official photo lineup. I'll have to head over to Miles eventually to see if he can identify any of them. If he does, we'll have to call in the DA and see what they have to say about getting a warrant," Roni explained.

"Is the lineup alone enough for a warrant?" John asked.

"Possibly not. But we're still waiting for the additional review that Roni's colleagues are doing into the evidence from the Hernandez suicide. If we're lucky, maybe we'll have more. Same with what the bomb squad and ATF are reviewing from the two bombings," Trey explained.

"Seems like there's still a lot to cover," Mia said with an exasperated sigh.

"There is, but don't lose hope," Roni said, and her best friend's words brought comfort, as did John's gentle touch.

"What do we do now?" Mia asked.

Roni jerked her thumb in Trey's direction. "The bottomless pit beside me is hungry again. I swear he's going to waddle down the aisle."

"Eating for two," he said and playfully nuzzled Roni's neck.

She scrunched her neck and said, "Get serious."

Trey swept his hand down his face and did just that, forcing a more thoughtful look on his features. "Get some rest while we wait for whatever Sophie and Robbie can dig up for the cloud account. Hopefully our police contacts will have more soon."

"I've reached out to Miles's phone provider to get his cell-phone data. Talk to you as soon as we have anything," Roni said in closing.

The video call ended, leaving Mia staring at John over the assorted papers on the table and the take-out menus.

"I know you're upset," he said and twined his fingers with hers.

"How did you guess?" she bit back sarcastically, but then shook her head and apologized. "I'm sorry. This is all so much to absorb."

"But you can do it. You always struck me as the kind of woman who could handle most anything," John said, attempting to reassure her.

She appreciated his words. "Thanks," she said and, as her stomach rumbled, she added, "I guess I'm more like Trey than I thought."

When John's stomach did a similar little noise, he laughed. "I guess we all are. Let's order something, eat and maybe take a break to watch a movie."

It sounded like a plan. While John organized all their papers and cleaned off the dining-room table, she flipped through the various menus and picked out one from a local Cuban restaurant that she recognized, since it wasn't all that far from Carolina's Surfside condo. Plus, she remembered that John loved his Cuban sandwiches so why not.

She placed the order for them and also got sandwiches for the guards on the property. Stepping out to Masters, she let him know to expect the delivery, and gave him the cash to pay for the meals. "If you need sodas or water, just let me know," she said and went back in to wait for the food.

HE HAD BEEN surprised when the tracker had begun to move from the SBS offices and toward South Beach. He had expected the cops would find it during their investigation of the shooting scene, but apparently, they hadn't.

Stupid cops. Typical, he thought, thinking of how he had avoided the MPs during his time in the army and after, when the cops had chased him and his gang members.

Was Miles heading to the Del Sol again? he wondered, hoping he was. He'd cased that place before when he'd tried to shoot Trey and his cop girlfriend.

But the tracker stopped well shy of the luxury hotel. From what he could see, the new location was in the South Pointe area, below Fifth Avenue and close to the park and water. Probably one of the high-end condo buildings in the area.

Determined to find out, he hopped into an older Mercedes he had "borrowed" from his cousin's used car lot the night before. Victor wasn't a big fan of his borrows, but since he often used his muscle to get car payments that were too far behind, his cousin couldn't complain too loudly.

He drove away from his mom's cinder-block home in Little Havana to the highway, racing to reach the location for the tracker in the hopes of discovering where Miles might be. Hoping John and Mia would be there also, so he could get rid of three birds with one stone.

Traffic was heavy, but moving nicely, and in no time, he was speeding across the causeway. His hands clenched the wheel in anger as he recalled messing up the attack on Ricky Gonzalez right by Jungle Island. Less than a mile or so up the road, he peered toward Palm Island, where the Gonzalez family had their gated home. He'd failed there, too, when their security guards had chased him away from the dock.

Fail, fail, fail, he thought and smacked the steering wheel in frustration. It had been the story of his life, from dropping out of high school, to his military service, and even the time in the gang and a local militia group. He'd never succeeded at anything unlike the Gonzalez family members, who seemed to be able to spin gold from whatever junk they touched.

But then again, he and his family hadn't had the advantage of being treated like heroes the way the Gonzalez patriarch had been. Every year they'd parade the eldest, Ramon, with the other Bay of Pigs heroes while his grandfather had rotted in a Cuban jail.

He was so lost in his angry thoughts he almost ran the red light at the end of the causeway and came to a screeching halt. Not good, especially since there was a police car parked across the way, hoping to catch anyone speeding off the causeway into South Beach.

The cop behind the wheel even looked his way, but he just played it cool and slowly turned down Alton

Road and toward South Pointe once the light turned green. He kept an eye on the tracker as he inched closer and closer to its position until he was finally in front of the Portofino Tower.

Not bad, Miles. Being his little brother's gofer had clearly paid off, he thought. From what he could tell, Miles was about ten or so floors up, and even though there was another tower nearby, taking a clear shot from that other building would be tough. Fisher Island was across the way, but getting on that private island was impossible. Only those invited by residents could board the ferry to get there.

It would have to be close and personal, he thought, smiling. There was something very rewarding about doing a kill that way. Bombs and bullets did the job, but watching the life fade from someone's eyes…

He pulled into the parking garage for the condo building, but as he entered, he caught sight of the SBS security guard positioned by the area for the elevator and stairs. The guard was armed and had his back to the wall, so he wouldn't have any element of surprise. He suspected that once he got past that one guard, there would be another inside.

Driving around the parking area, he tried not to attract too much attention as he pulled back out and found a spot in the visitor parking area of the nearby South Pointe Tower.

An hour passed and then a second and a third. Night had fallen hard with a bright full moon bathing the glass of the towers and making them glisten in the night sky.

Beautiful, but not good for any kind of sneak attack.

There was just too much light and Miles was clearly not going anywhere.

He'd have to wait for a better time. He was good at waiting. After all, his family had been waiting over sixty years for any kind of justice.

Chapter Sixteen

Mia's life was usually a whirlwind of activity revolving around her and Carolina, and the various events they attended. It was an exciting life and had proved to be financially rewarding once their lifestyle social-media accounts had taken off. "The Twins" as she and Carolina were affectionately known, were invited to most anything of importance in the Miami area. Those connections had also helped her assist her family on assorted cases, like the one that had first introduced her to John.

Now here she was, stomach full and feeling a little sleepy, tucked into his side while watching one of the movie classics he had in his collection. Not her usual nightlife.

With his high-tech existence, she hadn't figured him to be a black-and-white kind of guy, or have a home that made her feel like she was in a spa. The colors were calming, the furniture inviting. The moonlight shimmering on the pool outside cast patterns into the home, enveloping her with relaxing vibes. There was even a scent, clean and crisp, spilling from a diffuser in a far corner.

"This is nice," she said, snuggling deeper against him and closing her eyes.

"It is. I'm not used to just lying around," he said.

She half opened her eyes to peer at him. His head rested against the soft cushions of the leather couch. His eyes were closed, and a peaceful smile graced his lips. Those lips that had provided such pleasure the night before.

She inched up and dropped kisses along his jaw until she reached the side of his mouth. He half turned, met her mouth with his. Kissed her, his touch light at first, tender, but it wasn't enough. *Not nearly enough*, she thought and slipped into his lap, cradling his center with hers.

Heat built as he hardened beneath her and she did a roll of her hips, caressing him.

He gripped her hips hard with his hands, stilling the motion.

She drew away slowly to meet his gaze, questioning.

"I want you, Mia. Don't mistake why I'm stopping," he said as he brushed back a lock of her hair that had fallen forward and cupped her cheek.

"Why?" she pressed, wanting to understand.

"There's too much going on. Emotions are running high."

She laid her pointer finger against his lips, silencing him. "I'm not vulnerable, John. I know exactly what I'm thinking. What I'm feeling. What I want."

John blew out a breath and shook his head. "You're making this hard, Mia."

Grinning, she dragged her hips across him. "I hope so."

HIS BODY SHOOK from the force of the desire that blasted through his body with that sexy shift of her hips. But it was about more than passion for him. He wanted all of her. Wanted her, heart and soul, and while making

love to her now might be putting the cart before the proverbial horse, he couldn't stop denying her or himself.

He surged to his feet and carried her to his bedroom,
where he laid her on the bed and pushed a button by
the bedside to engage the privacy film on the wall of
windows. The film dimmed the moonlight, but it was
still bright enough to see her. See the crystalline fire
blazing in her sky-blue eyes, and her lips, those lips...

Bending, he kissed her, and she wrapped her arms
around his shoulders and drew him down to rest against
her on the bed. They kissed over and over. Touched, her
hands mobile along his back, holding him close.

He slipped his hand beneath the hem of her soft T-shirt
to find even softer skin there. Trailing his hands up her
body, he cupped her breast and she urged him on with
soft cries of need.

He gave her what she needed, but took as well, savoring the pleasure of her loving.

He didn't know how they got naked as clothes almost
flew off by themselves, but when skin hit skin, it was
impossible to stop. He couldn't deny that he needed her
more than he'd ever needed anything in his life.

Fumbling in the nightstand drawer, he yanked out a
condom and tore it open to fit it over himself. But as he
did so, Mia pushed him to his back to finish the task.
She covered his body with hers and took him into her
warmth. But she didn't move. She just straddled him
and gazed down at him, searching his features.

When she finally moved on him, he hoped that she
had found what she was looking for.

Each shift of her hips drove passion ever higher, until
her body tightened above him, and she arched her back,
calling out his name. But he wasn't done. He wasn't sure

he'd ever be done with her and as she fell back to earth, he shifted her beneath him and started the rhythm of their lovemaking again.

HER BODY WAS still trembling from her climax as he drove into her once more, slowly at first, but then with more command. Demanding, wanting her to join him as he fell over.

She cradled his shoulders and answered him, feeling the pull of his need. A need that she suspected was more than just physical, just as it was for her.

Passion grew ever more intense. She climbed with him, higher and higher. Grasping his shoulders, she inched up to rain kisses across his face. Urged him on with tender words. *"Mi amor,"* she said.

His body shook and he called out her name, on the edge of his release. With a few final strokes, he took them over the edge, calling her name.

"Mia. You're mine, Mia. Forever mine," he said as he kissed her and took her breath into him.

It slipped from her then. *"Te quiero."*

His body stilled and he leaned a hand on the mattress to lift off her slightly. "You love me?"

She silently cursed, sorry that she'd lost her control. It wasn't something she normally did, especially when she wasn't quite ready to admit it to herself.

Backtracking, she said, "I think I do. I mean, like you said, there's so much going on and emotions—"

He stopped her with a kiss, and she was grateful for that because it kept her mouth from saying any more stupid things.

When he finally broke away, he said, "I understand. You don't need to say more."

And yet she felt like she had to say more, especially as he rolled to his back, gathered her into his arms and pulled the sheets up over them. She tucked herself tight to his warmth and against the chill of the AC.

Even though the world was in turmoil, comfort and peace filled her in his arms, and little by little, sleep claimed her.

JOHN WASN'T USED to sleeping with women. It wasn't his kind of thing to sleep around no matter what the tabloids intimated about him.

Mia wasn't just any woman. She was beautiful, intelligent, brave… He could go on and on, but that would only make it harder when she left.

And she would leave despite the words that had slipped out of her mouth. He was just a nerdy computer programmer with too much money. Not the kind of man someone as vibrant and social as Mia would want.

But he'd accept this loving for now, short-lived as it might be.

Her body relaxed against him in little pieces, growing heavier as she drifted off. Long minutes later that soft little snore sounded in the quiet of the night, confirming she was fast asleep, but he couldn't join her. There were too many thoughts and ideas flitting through his head about what they had uncovered so far.

Too many thoughts that made him gently move away from her side, easing a pillow in his spot so she'd be less likely to notice his absence.

He searched the floor for his clothes, slipped into them and crept from the bedroom, closing the door behind him as not to wake her.

His laptop sat on the table, calling to him to get back

to work, as it did so often. Other than Miles, the laptop and his code had been his constant companions. But now he had Mia as well. At least for now, and he had to do whatever he could to protect her.

He sat and powered up the computer, then considered what else he could do and a vague memory came to him about some cell-network providers being hacked, possibly by the Chinese. Immediately a result popped up in his search engine and he read through the various articles, until he reached one that discussed that the hacks had obtained years' worth of call detail records. That information was exactly what he wanted and, digging deeper, it seemed various tech journals explained how the hackers had broken into the system to get the information.

But the article also mentioned how the National Security Agency had been collecting similar call detail records for millions of Americans. If they were still running the program, they might possibly have the information that Roni was trying to obtain from Miles's cell-phone provider.

Hacking the NSA would have way too many consequences if he was caught, but if that turned out to be his last resort, he'd do it to protect Mia and the rest of the Gonzalez family.

For now, he started off by hiding his own information with his VPN and other tools. Feeling safely screened from discovery, he repeated the steps done by the most well-known hackers to try and break into Miles's phone provider, searching their network for certain types of non-Windows servers that had more lax security and monitoring solutions in order to access the server. If he was successful, he'd use a password-spraying protocol he'd developed to break into the servers or maybe even find one of the back doors the hackers had left to let them reaccess the servers. But as he tried and tried again, it seemed as if this cell provider may have taken steps to protect against the hacks.

He was about to try another avenue when the snick of the door opening drew his attention to the bedroom. Mia stood there in only a T-shirt, her hair sleep-tousled and her blue gaze assessing as she glanced in his direction.

She walked over, stood behind him and wrapped her arms around him. When she saw what he was doing, she said, "Please, tell me you're not—"

"I am," he admitted. "I feel like I have to do something."

Hugging him tight, she said, "You're doing more than you know and you can't compromise all that you've worked for like this."

He put his hands on the table and stared at his screen. With a shrug, he said, "I haven't been able to break in."

"Good. Come back to bed and get some rest. We need to be fresh in the morning when we have more information," she said and smoothed a hand across his chest.

He glanced over his shoulder and met her sleepy gaze. "I wish I could be as optimistic about what we'll have in a few hours."

She whispered a kiss on his forehead. "Come back to bed."

Smiling tightly, he shut the laptop, rose and encircled her in his arms. "Let's go to bed."

DESPITE HER ASSERTIONS to John that they needed to get some rest, it had taken her a very long time to fall asleep. Once he was in bed beside her, he'd been sound asleep in only a few minutes, and she wondered if he'd trained himself to do that. She could picture him doing long hours at his computer and then dropping off to get some *z*'s before going back to work.

In a way she was used to it as well, thanks to the late nights she often kept with Carolina at their various social events. But she normally didn't end her nights with a very handsome man in her bed, contrary to what some might think.

She sighed as she recalled their lovemaking and the accidental slip of the tongue that was bound to complicate things beyond their already complicated state.

Shaking her head in chastisement, she busied herself with making coffee and rummaged through his cabinets and refrigerator to see what she could make for breakfast. She located some granola and yogurt, as well as eggs and cheese. *Enough for a healthy parfait and an omelet*, she thought.

She had just finished the parfaits and was whipping up the eggs when John strolled out of the bedroom, raking back the errant locks of his hair with his fingers.

"Good morning," he said. He walked to her side and hesitated for a second before dropping a tentative kiss on her cheek.

She understood his caution since she was feeling it, too, after the eruption of passion from the night before. But she didn't want that restraint between them. She wanted to see where this could go, so she leaned into him and kissed him without hesitation.

This time he answered her eagerly, meeting her mouth with his until they broke apart, breathless and staring at each other. "I'm not sorry about last night," she said.

"I'm not either," he said, but they didn't get to explore it further as the phone rang, warning that reality was intruding.

Chapter Seventeen

John hadn't been feeling optimistic the night before, but as Roni detailed the updates she'd gotten from her colleagues that morning, he finally felt some relief.

"The bomb squad and ATF have confirmed that similar materials and methods were used in the bombing at the Hernandez construction site and the car bomb," she said. "Both bombs contained fertilizer and gasoline. In the car bomb, the gasoline in the gas tank amplified the blast."

"If there is that connection, what about Hernandez's supposed suicide?" Mia asked, leaning forward to peer at her best friend on the video call.

Roni smiled. "We caught a break there as well. CSI found a partial print on the casing of one of the unfired bullets in the revolver. It will take them a few hours to clean up the print enough to run it through AFIS. Once they do, that may take another couple of hours to see if we have a match to anyone in the system."

The mention of the bullet prompted John to ask a question. "What about the bullets from the sniper?"

Roni shook her head. "Too damaged from impact and the shooter policed his brass on the rooftop. No prints on the rooftop door either."

One step forward, two steps back, he thought.

Trey's fiancée noticed his frustration and said, "We're closing the noose around him, John. You have to believe that."

He nodded. "What about the tracker? What do we do with that for now?"

It was Sophie who popped in with a report. "We're getting close to identifying the cloud account using the serial number on the tag and trying to reach it with fake location pings."

"Won't that alert the provider and make them disable the tag?" John queried.

Sophie and Robbie shared a look. "It might. That's why we're being very careful with how we're doing it."

It was ingenious and he admired their creativity. "If you ever want to leave SBS, let me know," he teased, earning smiles from the two siblings.

"What can we do in the meantime?" John asked, feeling useless because he had exhausted what he could do, absent illegally hacking into the cell-phone provider or the NSA. It also didn't escape his notice that he'd made it a *we* and not an *I* because Mia and he were partners in so many ways.

"We should have the call detail records in the next hour or so. It may be a lot to process manually, especially plotting the cell-tower locations," Trey said.

John nodded. "I'll process that data as soon as you send them," he said, paused and added, "What about Miles? What do we do about him?"

At the mention of his brother, Mia laid a hand on his shoulder to offer comfort, understanding it was still a raw wound.

Roni and Trey shared a look and Roni's lips tightened

into a harsh line. "I'm not sure we'll be able to protect him if the DA wants to press charges for what he's done, both the insider trading and the attack in your offices."

"I understand," John said with a dip of his head.

"If he reaches out to you, or if you reach out to him, tell him to sit tight and not to move the tracker," Trey said, and his cousins confirmed it by nodding.

"I'll let him know."

WILSON HADN'T MOVED from the night before. Or at least the tracker hadn't moved.

He'd done surveillance off and on until midnight, carefully driving around the area as not to draw too much attention to himself. He'd even passed a police car patrolling the area, but the cop hadn't blinked an eye as he drove by.

He scanned the tower and noticed the floor where the window shades and blinds were still drawn against the late-morning light. They'd been closed last night as well.

The snake was hiding in his hole, but for how long and why? he wondered. Had John Wilson caught on to the fact that Miles couldn't be trusted? Is that why he was still at home on a workday, or were the brothers afraid of another attack on their offices?

Regardless, Miles had to come out eventually, and when he did, he'd be ready.

RONI HADN'T BEEN kidding when she'd said that the call detail records would be too much to review manually, Mia thought. It had all seemed like gibberish to her until John had explained each item and what it meant. With little else to do, Mia was determined to get something useful from the information.

Wanting quiet because she'd realized that even a sitting John was like a teakettle about to boil, sometimes nervously bouncing his legs or tapping his feet, other times mumbling beneath his breath, she escaped to his office. However, she couldn't get to work right away since the photos, awards and other ephemera of John's life called to her from the wall units to the side of his desk. She laid down the call detail record reports they'd printed and casually strolled from one item to the next, taking in those tidbits from his life.

A framed photo of John with Miles and a woman she assumed was their mother. Miles had her sandy-colored hair, but John was almost a spitting image of the beautiful woman. She had a button nose that softened a face dominated by a strong chin and square jaw. It looked like the picture had been taken at some kind of graduation—college, she guessed.

In another photo, Miles and John stood in front of the door to the start-up John had sold several months earlier. Awards from charity organizations, mostly ones helping women in need, were mixed in with an assortment of books and technical manuals.

Returning to the desk, she set the report with Miles's call records in the center of the desk, grabbed a pen and highlighters, and started reviewing it. After barely an hour, her eyes were blurring from looking at the data, but she focused and decided to keep her attention on the columns with the cell-site data.

The same three cell sites seemed to be popping up for Miles and she wrote them down on a pad of paper and highlighted them, assuming that they were for things like the offices in downtown and the two brothers' homes. When she looked at the phone numbers being dialed from those cell sites, there seemed to be a lot of communication between John and Miles at the various locations. Not unexpected, since the two were working together.

Frustrated, she leaned back in the comfy leather executive chair and gazed out the wall of windows across the way. They faced the lush gardens that had been planted around the home and at the edges of the road, a well-manicured lawn and a central courtyard, where water spilled down tiered basins into a large pool. Flashes of gold and orange hinted that there were fish in the large lower basin.

Much like in the rest of the home, there was a decided zen feel to the room, what with the views of the garden and fountain, and the colors of the furniture, floor and walls in the office. It created a peaceful and relaxing feel that chased away some of the frustration raging inside her.

Returning to the papers, she flipped the pages until she got to the date and time when the attack had happened at John's old offices. She flagged it and noted something interesting: the cell site for the incoming call and Miles's phone at that time were the same. On top of that, the number hadn't been hidden.

The intruder had been close to the office, which made sense. Miles must have tipped him off as to when to fake the attack.

She wrote down the number reflected on the report, not that it would do much good. It was likely a burner phone. But she still went through the rest of the report, noting that there had been at least two other calls from that number to Miles prior to the attack, but none after.

"Bingo!" She heard John's voice from the other room and hurried out to where he was staring at the laptop.

"Good news?" she asked and peered at the laptop screen, which appeared to show a map of the area with clusters of dots in various areas.

He grabbed a remote, flipped on the television and cast his screen there.

Using a laser pointer, he highlighted the various areas and explained.

"I programmed the locations of the various cell towers and analyzed how many phone calls were made in the vicinity of those towers. You can see the larger circles, which indicate the volume of calls," he said.

"I eliminated calls that Miles and I made to each other," he said, and with the tap of a few keys, the circles diminished substantially, but there were still quite a few calls emanating from the downtown area with even more scattered circles in South Beach and Little Havana.

Holding her hands out in question, she said, "There are still too many other calls."

"THERE ARE, so I used my program to eliminate commonly called numbers, like ones to Versailles and other restaurants. The Del Sol, of course," John said and issued another command to the laptop.

"Wow. That got rid of a lot of them," Mia said with a breathy sigh.

"It did. I'm going to have the program make a list of the addresses for the remaining locations and compare it to the last known addresses for our various suspects,"

John said, and at that statement, Mia held up a finger and rushed off to his office.

She returned a few seconds later with the printed reports, where she had highlighted various items and a pad of paper with her notes.

"These are the cell-tower sites for calls made from what I think was the attacker to Miles. You should be able to confirm that against your data. I wrote down the dates and times as well and one of them matches up with the attack on your office," Mia explained.

"Good work. Once we have that, we'll send the analysis to SBS and see if they have any new info," he said. As he started to type, a knock came at the door.

"I'll get that," Mia said and raced off to answer the door.

A few seconds later, Mia's surprised gasp traveled across the room. "What are you doing here?"

John turned in his seat to look past Mia to where Miles stood at the door, the security guard at his side. Mia half turned to face him, her gaze questioning.

He joined her and jerked his head to let the guard know he could go back to his car. "Mia's right. We asked you to stay put."

Miles ran a shaky hand through his hair. "I was going stir-crazy. Let me help, John."

John looked past Miles and down the driveway to see if there were any other cars in the area. "Did you make sure you weren't being followed?" he asked.

His brother looked back toward the road and with a shrug and shake of his head, he said, "I don't think so."

"Dude, you need to be careful. Go home and stay put," John urged.

Miles looked from him to Mia and back to him. "You won't let me stay?"

His brother had stayed with John dozens of times after late nights of programming or partying, but that had been before, and things were different now. "I won't. We're working on things—"

Angrily, Miles jabbed a finger in each of their directions. "We're working? The two of you? What can she possibly do?"

He wanted to say "More than you've ever done" but that wouldn't be fair. His brother had done a lot for him, possibly even saved his life from his abusive father. Because of that, he tempered his response.

"I'm not sure you can help right now. Please go home. When we need you, we'll call. Text me when you get there," John said.

Miles looked between the two of them, and with an abrupt nod, he marched away to his car.

They stood there, watching the car drive down to the road and almost disappear from sight behind the thick foliage along the edge of the road.

Mia slipped her hand into his. "It'll be okay, John. *He'll* be okay," she urged.

Miles might be okay, but John wasn't sure he could ever trust his brother again and that filled him with sadness.

With a quick dip of his head, he squeezed her hand and said, "Let's get back to work."

HE HUNG FAR back from Miles's Lexus, not wanting to let the man know that he was being followed. It was relatively easy along A1A, with enough traffic to let him hide behind other cars as they drove northbound. But as they got into the Surfside area and he realized Miles was turning off to head to Indian Creek, he slowed considerably.

The island only had about forty or so homes and a golf course, so it would be tough to stay out of sight. But he wanted to know where John had his home. Where Mia would be hiding out with the tech multimillionaire and likely more vulnerable than the other family members in their gated and protected residences.

He slipped onto a side street as Miles continued across the bridge onto the island, then doubled back and onto the bridge, creating a good deal of distance from Miles. But he could still see that the Lexus had driven in the direction of the golf course.

He did the turn as well, moving slowly and surveilling the area to get a feel for it, so he would know the best way to make an escape.

Barely fifty yards ahead of him, Miles pulled into a driveway and excitement raced through him.

He contained himself, moving at a normal pace past the driveway, so as not to draw attention.

A few homes down, the land on either side of the road opened into grassy areas that signaled the start of the golf course.

He kept on going and turned into the parking lot for the country club, where he parked and yanked out his phone to get a map of the area. He muttered a curse as he realized the only road on the island dead-ended at either end and the bridge was the only way on and off the island.

Any attack would take a great deal of planning, he thought and drove away, his pace measured again, especially as he neared the driveway where he had seen Miles turn in.

There was heavy foliage all along the area by the road, but he thought he caught sight of a car near the mouth of the driveway and two other vehicles parked by the front door. They screamed of being cop cars, at least two of them, so it might not be easy to get up close for a kill, the way he liked it. But there was also a lot of open space that might give him a clear shot from the golf course.

If that was all he could get, he'd take it.

IT WAS IMPOSSIBLE to miss the dejected set of John's shoulders and the misery in his gaze.

Mia understood. She didn't know how she would handle it if one of her siblings had behaved like Miles. But then again, she couldn't imagine that anyone in her family ever would.

She left John at the table working on his computer and walked into the kitchen to make some coffee. As she did so, her phone chirped to say she had a message.

How r u holding up? Carolina texted.

Guilt filled her that she hadn't really kept her cousin and best friend in the loop. Because of that, she called Carolina.

"Hola, amiga," she said as her cousin answered.

"Hola, prima. Mami and I saw the news about the explosion, and we were so worried."

"I'm so sorry that I didn't call, but things have been too crazy," Mia said in apology.

"I know. Besides we have that twin thing, so I knew you were okay," Carolina teased, helping to ease her guilt.

"Gracias. I'm glad you and *Tia* Elena are away and

safe," she said, and in the background, she could hear her aunt calling out a greeting.

Carolina blew out a sigh that carried across the line. "I wish there was some way we could help."

"Me, too, but for now staying away is a big help," she said, and it made her think of Miles's visit. Worry filled her that he hadn't been careful and that the killer may have tracked him to John's home.

"We'll stay at the spa as long as you need, but if that should change—"

"We'll let you know," Mia said and ended the call. But no sooner had she hung up than her phone was ringing again with a call from Trey.

His voice was excited as he said, "Sophie and Robbie think they may have gotten the cloud-account name."

"Let me put you on speaker so John can hear," she said and hurried over to John's side. She tapped on the speaker key, set the phone on the table and said, "What can you tell us?"

"I've got Sophie and Robbie here as well," Trey said.

A second later, Sophie came across the line. "We only had it for a second before the system's security shut us down, but we got it. *JMMADDTRAX*."

"JMADDTRAX?" Mia said, wanting to make sure she had understood.

Sophie spelled it out so there would be no confusion and after she did so, Mia peered at John to see if it made sense to him because it didn't mean anything to her.

He shook his head. "Not a clue," he said but immediately jumped on his laptop.

"It didn't mean anything to us either and an internet search didn't get us any hits," Trey advised.

John gestured to his laptop so she could see that he was also drawing a blank.

With a shrug, she said, "Could it be initials? Some kind of nickname?"

"Or tracks as in motocross, or lay down music tracks or even racks for something," Robbie mused.

"We'll have to play around with it. Can you guys do that as well?" Trey asked.

"Will do, but in the meantime…have you heard from anyone about the partial print?"

"Not yet, but we hope to have it soon. What about you? Any progress on the call detail records?" her brother said.

John and she shared a look and then John said, "I've plotted where all the calls either originated or terminated, and I'm working on eliminating as many as I can. Mia put together some info as well and we'll hopefully have something for you in another couple of hours."

"Great. Let's touch base again before dinner. I'd love to get together to share ideas, but I don't want to clue anyone to where you might be," her brother said.

The look she shared with John this time was troubled. "We already had a guest today. Miles came by, but we sent him back home and told him to sit tight."

A long silence drifted across the line. "That worries me," Trey said calmly. Too calmly.

"We have the guards here, Trey. No need to worry," Mia said, trying to dispel any fears he might have.

"If he was followed—"

"He wasn't, we don't think," Mia said.

Another awkward silence followed but then Trey said, "I'll make sure the guards are on high alert. We'll talk to you later."

Once he'd hung up, Mia sat beside John, who met

her gaze, clearly troubled. "Trey's right. What if some-one followed Miles?"

"You have a security system that goes to a central station, right?" she said and gestured to the keypad by the front door.

When he nodded, she said, "We have three armed guards on the grounds and bulletproof glass."

"But he's a sniper who knows how to make bombs," John replied quickly.

She didn't argue with him because she couldn't. But they were safe for now and so was Miles, who had texted to confirm he had arrived at his condo.

Turning the conversation away from that, she said, "If *JMMADDTRAX* stands for something else, what could it be?"

"Like you said before, it could be a lot of different things," John said with a shrug.

"Too many combinations," she said.

"92,378, if we start rearranging all ten letters," he said nonchalantly, but at her surprised look he shrugged and added, "I'm kinda good with math."

"I should have figured you were some kind of ge-nius," she said.

He grimaced. "You don't know how I hate that word. Besides, we don't want to look at all the combinations. Just ones that maybe mean something."

Because he obviously didn't want to talk about his genius skills, she said, "I guess we start searching for those combos."

He nodded. "Let's start searching for any references to 'mad tracks.'"

"Two real words that someone may have changed for their username?" she asked.

With another nod, he said, "Maybe 'mad tracks' was already taken. Sometimes people add numbers but other times they just add letters."

If anyone would know about the behavior of computer users, it would be John, Mia thought.

The first search got immediate results, returning dozens of hits for a very popular video game. "The gang member is a gamer?" she said, speculating.

"If he is, maybe it's also his gang-member name. Roni can probably have her people run that," John said, and Mia jotted it down with their notes.

They kept at it, thinking of possible word combinations and variations, and searching on the internet for anything that would point them in the direction of one of the possible suspects they had previously identified.

As they were about to try another set of variables, Trey phoned again.

"You have news?" Mia asked.

"I do, but it isn't good."

Chapter Eighteen

John watched the faces of the various Gonzalez family members on the video call as Roni ran through the information she'd been given about the partial print.

She screen-shared a rap sheet for a possible suspect. "AFIS spit out Jaime Cruz based on the partial print. Cruz was on my list of favorites and high on John's list of possible suspects."

"That's a good thing, isn't it?" John asked and looked at the report his program had produced based on the information Roni had provided. According to his program, there had been an eighty-percent probability that Cruz was involved in the attacks.

"It is except for one problem—Cruz was killed six months ago in a gang-related shooting," Roni advised.

Silence filled the air and the faces of the family members turned stony with that revelation.

From the corner of his eye, he caught sight of Mia's worried features. "He's been dead for six months but somehow his fingerprint is on a bullet casing?"

"Can you say 'bizarro'?" Robbie said.

"The gun must have gone to someone who knew Cruz," Trey said and brought up the photos of a few of their other suspects on the screen. "These are other gang members who may have known him and were on our list."

John skimmed his finger down his report, checked the probability numbers and shook his head. "These are all low probability."

"It's what we have to go on so far," Roni said with a frown and continued. "I was waiting to ask Miles to come in for a lineup until we had the result from the partial print, but I think it may be time to have him take a look at these other suspects."

John wasn't so sure about that. "I trust your judgment, but...can we hold off until tomorrow? We're still working on this cloud-account info, and I should have more for you on the cell-site locations soon."

Roni slipped an uneasy glance at Trey, but then reluctantly nodded. "Okay, tomorrow. I'm going to reach out to my contacts and see if they know who Cruz's friends in the gang were. Relatives also. If I get anything, I'll pass it on."

"Sounds good and thanks for everything, Roni. We appreciate it," Mia said, and John ended the call.

"Dead." John sighed in frustration. "Our one and only suspect is dead."

MIA UNDERSTOOD HOW he felt. She'd experienced the same emotions more than once when she'd been involved in one of her family's investigations. But this was worse because this was way more personal.

She slipped her hand into his. "Let's take a break. I'll make us dinner."

He raised his hand in a stop gesture. "Let me. I like to cook."

"Really? A liberated man. I like that," she said and

playfully tugged on his hand to pull him from the table and into the kitchen area.

Mia took a spot by the counter as John opened the fridge, pulled out several things and walked over to the counter.

"Stir-fry, okay?" he asked and laid an assortment of vegetables and a skirt steak on the granite.

She nodded. "I'd like that. Want me to make some rice?"

"Sure," he said and got to work, cutting and chopping while she rinsed the rice and got it cooking.

While he did the stir-fry, she set the table, and opened a bottle of white wine. After pouring them each a glass, she returned to John's side and set the glass by where he was working. Leaning against the counter, she watched as he added the carrots and broccoli to the wok and gave a stir.

He stopped to take a sip and smiled. "Tasty," he said and raised the glass to clink it against hers.

She grinned. "You have an excellent wine cellar. Did you pick the wines yourself?"

With a self-deprecating smile, he shook his head. "No way. I wouldn't know Moët from Mad Dog, but I'm trying to learn."

"You get an A for this one," she said and turned down the heat on the rice as it started to boil, setting it to a low simmer. The rice would finish cooking and steam so it wouldn't get sticky.

"That's praise coming from you, princess," he said, dampening her mood a little.

"Not a princess, remember. There are things I had to learn, too," she admitted.

He set aside his wooden spoon and peered at her. "I'm

sorry. I know you haven't always had it easy. Maybe we can learn together," he offered an apology.

Grinning, she said, "I'd like that. How about I stir while you keep on chopping?"

He nodded and together they cooked the meal like a well-choreographed ballet, and in no time, they were sitting at the table, eating the delicious meal they'd pre- pared.

She must have been hungry since she devoured her first plate and so did John. She served them the last of the rice and stir-fry, and after, they cleaned up and loaded everything into the dishwasher, then settled onto the couch to finish their wines before returning to work.

They sat there quietly, lost in their thoughts and their company as they sipped the wine.

The ideas in her brain were like a kaleidoscope, whirling and twirling, multicolored, as she tried to slip all the different thoughts into seemingly logical cate- gories. But there were just too many loose threads that refused to be woven into any kind of pattern, so she focused on one.

"What if the *JM* aren't the initials?" she suggested and finished off her wine.

"You're saying the initials are *JMM* and we should search *ADDTRAX*?" he asked.

She shook her head. "No, I mean what if the start of the name is actually *JMMADD*? I know it's weird—"

"No weirder than *MADDTRAX* and that's gotten us nowhere. Stay here," he said and hopped off the couch to grab his laptop.

She tucked herself close as he placed his computer on his lap and did the search on *JMMADD*.

"I'll be damned," he said as the results came up.

"Wow, what are the odds that's not a coincidence?" she said as she saw result after result. *JMMadd* had been the code name of a secret CIA airfield in Guatemala used as part of the Bay of Pigs invasion.

"Didn't your grandfather take part in the Bay of Pigs?" John asked.

She nodded. "He was a member of the brigade." Pointing to his computer. "Try *JMMTrax*."

He did, but when he got no hits, he changed it to *JMTrax* and sure enough, a slew of results popped up, also linking the term to the failed invasion of Cuba that had been engineered by the CIA and scuttled by President Kennedy.

Puzzled, Mia said, "It's been over sixty years. What connection could the Bay of Pigs have to what's happening?"

JOHN WAS AS puzzled as Mia. "It can't be someone who was involved in the invasion. They'd be like what? Eighty years old?"

"*Mi abuelo*—my grandfather—is 87. I'm not sure how many survivors are still alive, but if they are, they'd all probably be in their late 70s, 80s and even 90s. Our attacker was young," Mia said.

"He was. If this is a real connection we've discovered, it's likely that our attacker is a 'grand,'" he said, using air quotes and continued. "Grandchild, grandnephew. Our generation."

Mia held her hands up as if in pleading, trying to understand. "But why? It happened sixty years ago."

"I don't know enough about it to say, Mia. But I think it's time to get everyone involved. Maybe even call your grandfather," John said.

Mia grabbed her phone, dialed Trey and explained what they had discovered.

John heard the murmur of his voice in agreement and when she hung up, she said, "Trey is going to set up a video call."

When a familiar tone announced the incoming call, he answered and cast the image to the television screen to get a clearer view of the Gonzalez family members.

Mia scooted closer to him so that she'd appear in the video as well.

"We think we've figured out the meaning of *JM-MADDTRAX*," John said and quickly explained what they had unearthed.

The reaction of the other Gonzalez family members matched Mia's earlier reaction.

"That can't be," Trey said.

"But that's so long ago," Sophie said.

Robbie added, "Almost ancient history."

Mia shook her head, chastising her cousin. "That's because you two mostly grew up in the DC area. In Miami, it's still important, still a wound to a lot of Cuban exiles."

"Mia's right. When the sixtieth anniversary of the invasion happened in 2021, the veterans of the brigade were honored by the governor and others. That history is almost as alive today as it was sixty years ago," Trey warned his cousins.

Sophie lifted a hand to her chest in a gesture of apology. "So sorry. But if this is related to Grandfather Ramon, do we have to worry about him being attacked?"

"John can run that through his program to get the probability, but since *abuelo*'s staying put on Palm Island, *abuela* and he should be safe," Trey said.

"I will run it," John said, but as he went to the dashboard, he realized he already had a hit on an earlier operation he'd been running. Muttering a curse, he said, "I've got to finalize this dashboard."

"What is it, John?" Sophie asked, dark eyebrows furrowed with worry.

John waved off her concern. "I have the analysis of the cell-tower sites related to all those calls. It looks like there are about half a dozen locations where the calls were made. I'll send you the information so you can review it."

Sophie and Robbie nodded. "We will. We're still working on that cloud account and the tracker. It's still active and sending signals. Maybe to one of those cell towers on your list," Sophie said.

Mia said, "If there is a connection to *abuelo* and this stalker is mad at the family—"

"We can ask Ricky to chime in on that and maybe give us a profile," Trey said.

Mia spoke up again. "The gang member is related to someone connected to the invasion somehow. Speaking of gang members, where's Roni?"

"At the precinct chatting up her colleagues about any connections to Cruz," Trey explained.

"If this is family-related, doesn't it make sense that it's not just a gang member? That it could be someone in Cruz's family?" Mia asked.

"It does make sense and we can start doing a search for relatives who might fit the other requirements," Sophie said.

Trey slapped the top of his desk. "Sounds like we each have something to do. I'll reach out to Ricky and

Roni, Sophie and Robbie will keep working on the tracker and get started on any family ties—"

"We'll work on those also and any connections to our list of suspects. We'll also keep hammering at those cell sites," John said and peered at Mia from the corner of his eye.

She nodded to confirm it and so did her brother and cousins, who signed off one by one, leaving him staring at the image of him and Mia on the big screen. He signed off as well, faced Mia and said, "I guess we have our work cut out for us."

"We do. I'll go make some coffee."

HE HAD THOUGHT an attack would be difficult, but the more that he researched it, the more he realized it was nearly impossible.

Only one way off and on the island.

The house was on the southern-most tip, and while he had a clear shot at the front of Wilson's house from the golf course, the main living areas of the home were in the back as far as he could tell from the real-estate photos he'd tracked down on the internet.

Stillwater Drive was across the way, but the angle was all wrong.

The other way to approach the property was via Biscayne Bay, but the water would have to be like glass for him to use his 50 cal for a shot or any other rifle for that matter. Not to mention that the area was popular with boaters, creating all kinds of wakes to disrupt his aim.

He could steal a Sea-Doo, as he'd done in the past, but if there was a guard near the dock, he'd have to neutralize him as well. He already had one body to answer for, but that had been easy. Jorge Hernandez hadn't expected his hired hand to turn on him.

A paid security guard, especially one from the SBS group, would be harder to take down but he liked a challenge.

Pulling up a street view, he continued planning.

Chapter Nineteen

It didn't surprise Mia that quite a number of the areas identified via the cell-tower sites were in Little Havana. If the killer had a connection to the Bay of Pigs veterans, they were more than likely Cuban, and Miles had said the caller had an accent. While many Cubans had moved into other neighborhoods, there were still quite a number of Cubans in Little Havana and the nearby areas.

"Could you zoom in on the part of the map in Little Havana?" she said, and he did, revealing four different circles, which identified the general area from where the calls had originated. Despite John eliminating calls that he and his brother had made to the restaurant, a circle still covered the area for the location on *Calle Ocho*.

Running her finger from the restaurant to the other locations, she said, "You could walk these easily."

John nodded. "For sure. Go and get a morning *cafecito*. Run by at lunch hour to get a Cubano."

"A regular. Someone no one looks at twice. Just a neighborhood guy walking up to *La Ventanita* to get his coffee or a sandwich. Even Miles, if he went to pick up something and made a call from there," Mia said and leaned back in the chair, considering that possibility. She circled her finger around the area and said, "What else is around there? A bank or something else with a CCTV?"

With a shrug, John pulled up a street view for the area and swiveled around to examine the street. "Nothing here, but maybe farther up," he said and did the virtual walk away from the Versailles restaurant. Across the street was another eatery, *La Carreta*, with its kitschy wagon wheel on the side of the building. But directly across the street was a bank with an ATM machine that faced *Calle Ocho*.

"That's a good thing, isn't it?" Mia said, leaning close to confirm what she was seeing. A second later, a darker green circle appeared on the screen in that area.

John gestured to it. "You gave me the info for the cell-site location for the number we think is from the killer. This is where the computer says the call was likely made."

"We have the time it was made. Roni should be able to get the ATM footage from that location," Mia said and was about to call her best friend when John stopped her.

"Let's map the locations of the other two calls," he said and a second later, he zoomed out on the map to show where the two dark green circles were visible.

One of the locations was less than a dozen blocks away, on Flagler. "He could walk there," Mia said, pointing to the location.

As he had done before, John displayed the street view, but other than a few small stores and a used-car lot, there was nothing that would give them any information. But something niggled at Mia's consciousness about the location.

"Can you pull up the last one again? By the bank?"

she asked and as he did so, she noticed it immediately. "There's a bus stop in front. I think I saw one at the other location as well."

He flipped back to the other location and sure enough, there was another bus stop in front of the used-car lot.

"That's too much coincidence," he said and immediately checked the last location, which was in the downtown area, close to their old offices and the SBS building.

"That call from downtown is not far from our offices," Mia said, but then shook her head. "If this guy doesn't have a car and keeps stealing them, that just ups the likelihood that he gets caught while driving one. I'm not sure he's that stupid."

"I agree. From what I remember of your other recent cases, he has to have wheels of some kind."

"The bus route—I think it's the 208, by the way. Just coincidence?" Mia offered, eyes narrowed as she processed the information.

John likewise considered it but couldn't say. "I'm going to run this through the program. Let's take a look at something else, though."

He typed in the address for the downtown location and displayed the street view. Swiveling around to inspect the area, he stopped and tapped the screen. "Another bank right across from where the call was made."

"We need to have Roni get the ATM footage from those two areas at the time the calls were made," Mia said and texted her friend.

Need ur help. Emailing deets.

Got it, Roni texted back.

Mia almost collapsed into the chair, feeling like a

weight had been lifted from her now that there was finally some progress on the case.

"We did good work," John said as he relaxed against the dining-room table. He gestured to his laptop and said, "It will take a few minutes for the probability and the family search may take hours. I don't know about you, but I'd like to stretch and maybe get some fresh air."

Mia eyed the back patio with both longing and trepidation. They'd be exposed out there, but it wasn't as bright as it had been yesterday, with the full moon, and the landscaping provided some privacy from the guard positioned near the waterfront. Not to mention that there was nothing but Biscayne Bay behind them for some distance. The closest land was the narrow spit of land for the homes by Stillwater Park and that was way off to the left.

Hopping to her feet, she held her hand out to John. "I'd like that. Just a short walk. Some fresh air."

JOHN SET ASIDE his laptop, slipped his hand into hers and stood. Together they walked toward the patio doors, and he slid one open. For parties and in nicer weather, the immense glass doors folded away to create a seamless open space between the living-room area and the outdoor-patio area.

Thick ground cover and the leaves of colorful caladiums around the garden spilled onto the edges of the travertine patio tiles, while lush elephant ears, with their immense leaves, provided privacy at the edges of the gardens. Here and there, taller papyrus swayed with the night breeze, and oleander and bougainvillea flowers provided pops of color against the deep greens and wood of his home. Jasmine scented the night air, and he breathed the smell in deeply.

They strolled along the patio and, seeing the guard down at the dock, pushed a little farther toward the edge of the pool, lost in their thoughts. Eventually they turned back toward the house and the patio.

"You have a beautiful home," she said as he guided her to a large chaise longue, where they lay down, hidden from sight by the lush greenery around the space.

It *was* beautiful. Feeling like it was time to share more with her, especially when she snuggled into his side as if it was just the normal thing to do, he said, "It's the first place I can really call home."

She hesitated for a moment, but then said, "I know it wasn't easy for you what with your dad and everything."

He nodded. "It wasn't. I try not to remember only… you don't want to throw out the good with the bad and there was good there. My mom was the best. Miles, too."

She stiffened beside him. "I get it, Mia. He betrayed me. Brought the devil right into our home, but…he's the only family I have left."

"I understand, only…you may forgive him, but the authorities might not," she said and stroked her hand across his chest.

The authorities wouldn't be too happy with his insider trading, especially since he had manipulated the stock's price with his leak. But he didn't want to talk about Miles.

"What do you see yourself doing in five years?" he said and hated that it sounded so businesslike and impersonal.

"Why? Are you hiring?" she teased back with a laugh.

"I'm not really good at people skills. I'm better with machines," he replied with a chuckle.

She shifted to lie closer and nuzzled the edge of his jaw with her nose. "I think you're really good with people, John. Especially me," she whispered before kissing him.

He answered her kiss, opening his mouth to her, urging her body over his to lie against his length. The kisses were soothing at first, but slowly deepened, demanding more with each breath they took.

HE WAS HARD against the softness of her midsection and dampness flooded her center at the memory of making love to him the night before.

She wanted to make love with him all night long. Maybe even for the next five years, or ten, or more, she thought but couldn't say.

Instead, she slipped from the lounge, stood beside him and grabbed hold of his hand. "Come inside. I don't want the guard to see us get *nekkid*," she replied with a laugh.

He grinned, his smile bright even in the dim light. Jumping to his feet, he grabbed hold of her hand and tugged her into the house, stopping only to close and lock the patio doors.

Once the doors were secured, and his alarm system was set, they almost ran into the bedroom, then fell on the bed, laughing and kissing. They tossed aside clothing playfully until he was leaning over her, suddenly serious.

"I can't believe you're mine," he said, revealing his pain again. Not only that of his family's past, but also of what he was. A genius. A loner, but not by choice, she suspected, recalling how well he had meshed with her family in such a short time.

"You are a part of me, John. Part of me and my family. Never doubt that," she said and rose up to kiss away the hurt.

JOHN TOOK HER kiss into him, let her love wash over him. As much as this house was now his home, he couldn't imagine Mia not being a part of it either.

But he tempered what he wanted to say because of all that was happening and might be clouding their emotions. Instead, he showed her with his kisses and body what he felt for her. How he cared for her, revered her.

She was everything he'd never imagined possible for himself. A bright and caring woman. A ready-made family because he had no doubt that the Gonzalez family was a package deal and surprisingly, he wanted to embrace it. Embrace the kind of family he'd never really had.

As passion rose, he opened his heart and body to her, holding nothing back. He wanted her to know just how precious she was to him.

Together they tumbled over and lay there in the aftermath of their loving, content. Quiet.

But soon the *ding-ding-ding* of their phones interrupted the peaceful lull, reminding them that they had work to do.

With a final kiss and a promise for later, they gathered their clothes to answer the calls demanding their attention.

SOPHIE AND ROBBIE had gone on one of the genealogy sites to try and collect the names of Jaime Cruz's family members. His grandparents were both gone, but they had confirmed that Cruz's maternal grandfather had taken part in the Bay of Pigs. Cruz's parents and three siblings were still alive. Add to that four aunts and uncles, as well as over a dozen first cousins.

John's list, which he had pulled from not just those sites, but a variety of public databases, also included a number of second cousins.

"That's a lot of people," Mia said with a heavy sigh.

"But the connection is on his maternal side," John said, immediately zeroing on that connection.

Ricky, who had been pulled in for this discussion to offer a profile said, "I agree with John. If there is anger at our family, probably for some imagined wrong, it's likely that whoever is behind it is on that side of the family, since that was the grandfather involved in the Bay of Pigs."

With a few keystrokes, John eliminated any family solely on Cruz's paternal side. "That cuts it back substantially. The grandfather's name was Carrera. Do you think your grandfather might remember him?"

Trey nodded. "*Abuelo* may be 87, but he's still sharp. It's late though, so it may have to wait until morning."

"What about *Papi*? Would he know?" Ricky asked.

"Maybe. I'll reach out to him, but maybe we can do some digging on the internet," Trey said.

Beside him, Mia reached for some of the papers from their earlier searches. Flipping through the pages, she said, "We have two Cruzes on the list of gang members but no Carreras."

John gestured to the numbers besides their names. "Those two are low probability. Nothing that says they have the skills to build bombs or be expert shots or work in the downtown area buildings."

Roni jumped in to offer her opinion. "My guys say these are just two low-level gofers in the gang and not anyone they see as a threat for violence."

"Two steps forward and one step back," Mia muttered from beside him.

"It's what we have to work on," Trey said, clearly resigned to following those leads.

"We'll get to work on it," John said, and everyone chimed in with their agreement, but not enthusiastically.

He understood. They'd expended so much energy and still only had a few pieces of the puzzle. But there were more and more pieces and he had to stay optimistic that soon they'd have the complete picture.

"John?" Mia asked at his prolonged silence.

"We have more than we think we do. We're just not seeing the forest for the trees," he said and offered her a reassuring smile.

"I'd like to take an axe to those trees," she joked.

He had just the axe to use. "I'm going to run all these names and all this data through the program."

Chapter Twenty

While John was using his program to pull data for all the various family members and figure out the probabilities for who might be behind the attacks, Mia decided to tackle it in another way: by finding out as much as she could about the failed invasion.

Her *abuelo* had sometimes shared stories, but not often. It had obviously been a very painful episode in his life between the actual battle, the imprisonment that had followed and the sense of betrayal that still lingered for so many Cubans even to this day.

Jumping on the internet while John worked beside her in bed, she pored over various accounts of the invasion and the aftermath, keeping in mind what her brother Ricky had said about someone harboring a grudge for some imagined wrong.

A wrong that had happened on the battlefield? she wondered, but from what she could see, the bulk of the stories were about the bravery of the men and how they had fought to the very last bullet before being taken captive.

Something in prison? Over a thousand men had spent twenty months in a Cuban prison until the United States had brokered a deal, providing fifty-three million dollars in food and medicine in exchange for their release in December of 1962.

Her *abuelo* had never mentioned anything at all about the prison and what might have happened there. Asking him might awaken emotional memories.

She hated the thought of doing that. She loved her *abuelo*. Looked up to him as a hero who had fought so hard for freedom and to give them all a better life.

John passed a finger across her brow, soothing the furrows there. "You're upset."

"It is upsetting. I'm so removed from this part of my family's past… Now I have to face it, embrace it, but it could be hurtful. Especially for *mi abuelo*."

"Hopefully we can avoid that," he said.

She nodded and murmured, "Hopefully. Do you have anything yet?"

"I have the list and one suspect who's slightly higher than the others on the list, but nothing earth-shattering. What about you?"

"Nothing about the Carrera grandfather. He's on the list of prisoners, but that's about it."

"Maybe it's time to make a call to one of the daughters?" John asked.

She nodded, but it was late. Too late to call someone, but suddenly her own phone chirped to warn of an incoming call.

Trey. She swiped to answer, worried that he was calling so late.

"What's up?"

"Can you get John? I'd like for him to hear this as well," he said.

Heat swept up her cheeks and she held up a finger to ask John to remain silent. "Sure," she said, then counted to ten to make it seem like they weren't lying together in bed and tapped on the speaker.

"He's here," she said.

"Great. I spoke to *Papi* to see if he knew anything about the Carrera family. He said that he'd met the grandfather at some of the reunions of the Bay of Pig survivors. He also met the two daughters as well," Trey said.

"And?" Mia pressed, impatient to get to the important bits.

"It turns out that Carrera wasn't one of the men released in 1962. No one knows why, but Fidel kept him in prison for another fifteen years. Carrera was eventually released as part of some kind of exchange for a man the US had identified as a Cuban spy."

"I've spent most of the night reading up on it and didn't see anything about something like that," Mia said, imagining how the family must have felt having a loved one imprisoned for so long.

"Apparently it was all kept low-key because it involved national security. *Papi* wouldn't even have found out about it if one of his daughters hadn't accidentally spilled the beans at one of the reunions," Trey advised.

"Fifteen years in a Cuban prison. That couldn't have been easy," John said.

It was impossible to miss the harsh sigh that Trey let out before he said, "And it apparently wasn't easy for the family here either. With Carrera imprisoned, it was hard to get established the way *abuelo* did. Ricky said this might be for an imagined wrong and I totally see how a family member could think that.

"Their grandfather—because we know the person who's doing this is younger—rots in jail while the family flounders here. The grandfather gets released and there's no hero's welcome for a number of reasons," Mia offered.

"First, there's the national security aspect, but also, it's fifteen years later. People are thinking about other things. Some had even forgotten about the invasion, others were trying to move on with their lives," John mused.

"Cubans don't forget much about Fidel, but you're right that for some who are younger, it's not as emotional as it is for their parents and grandparents," Trey said.

A long silence filled the room as they all thought about what Trey had just revealed.

John finally broke the silence. "Seems like the two Cruzes have to top the list, no matter how low probability they might be."

"I agree, but right now, we have no proof of anything. Roni is going to ask her guys to keep an eye on them," Trey said.

"Maybe those ATMs we identified will give us some video that might help," Mia reminded him.

"Maybe. We'll touch base in the morning. Try to get some rest," her brother said and hung up.

Mia laid her phone on the nightstand and tucked her laptop on its shelf. "I can't imagine holding a grudge for so long."

John likewise laid his laptop on the nightstand next to him and tucked her into his side. "I wish I could say that I didn't but…"

He didn't have to finish for her to know what was bothering him. She faced him, reached up and cupped his cheek. "Miles. He's had a gripe with you for a while."

With a grimace, he said, "Years, apparently, and I didn't see it."

She eyeballed him and he shrugged sheepishly. "Okay, I had some reservations after the leak, but who wants to believe that your only family is screwing you?"

"No one, but he's not your only family now. You have me and the rest of the crew," she said, then leaned forward and kissed him.

As they slipped down into bed, she held him close, wanting to heal his hurts. As he held her, peace settled over her, but she knew it wouldn't be a lasting peace until they stopped whoever was trying to kill her and her family.

She was impatient for it to be over, but if she'd learned one thing from Trey it was that impatience could be deadly. They would have to bide their time until tomorrow and whatever new information that day would bring.

JOHN WOKE UP with a headache after a night filled with memories of his father, Miles and cars for some reason.

He sat up on the edge of the bed, raked his fingers through his hair and glanced at the empty spot on the bed where Mia had been sleeping beside him. From the kitchen came the sounds of her puttering around and the blessed smell of coffee.

I'll need buckets of it to get through the day, he thought and massaged his temples to drive away the pounding in his head.

"You okay?" Mia asked as she walked over and handed him a cup of coffee.

"I didn't sleep well. It happens sometimes when I'm trying to work through a coding problem...and you snore," he teased. He accepted the mug from her and took a bracing sip.

She chuckled and sat beside him. "I could sleep in the guest room."

"Being next to you was the best part of the night," he said and leaned over to kiss her.

She tasted of her minty toothpaste and coffee, and as she dug her hand into his hair to hold him close, they kissed for long minutes until they reluctantly broke apart.

"I could get used to this every morning," he said.

"I could, too," she admitted and dropped another kiss on his lips before popping to her feet. "I made breakfast. Come and eat. I feel like this is going to be a long day."

Feeling the same way, he grabbed his T-shirt from the floor, slipped it on and followed her to the breakfast bar in the kitchen, where she had laid out place settings on the granite counter.

Mia worked at the stove, gave a last stir to the eggs and came over a minute later to serve them. She followed up by bringing over buttered toast and crispy slices of bacon.

"Looks good," he said and dug in, hungry despite the headache, but it lingered.

Mia must have sensed it. "Can I get you aspirin or something?"

He shook his head. He didn't think aspirin would drive away the thoughts unsettling him. "Just some weird things in my brain."

"Like what?" she asked.

Appreciating that she was trying to help him, he said, "Thoughts about my family and cars for some reason."

She grinned mischievously. "Missing the Lamborghini?"

He barked out a laugh. "I don't even know how I'm going to explain that to the insurance company," he said and forked up some of the eggs.

"Maybe that's why you're thinking about cars, only... We were talking about buses and cars yesterday. Didn't we also see a used-car lot in one of the street views?"

He scrunched his eyes tight, trying to recall the image. "I'm not sure but let's do the search again."

Suddenly eager to get back to their investigations, they scarfed down their breakfast.

John grabbed his mug and worked while Mia loaded the dishwasher.

He opened his laptop and immediately noted that his program had finished the analysis of the various family members, but there hadn't been much of a change from the probabilities they'd had days ago. The two Cruzes who were gang members had the highest scores, but as everyone had noted, they both seemed to lack the requisite skills to carry out the attacks. None of the other family members had set off whistles.

With the words on the screen jumbling together as his head continued to pound, he printed the report so he could take a closer look later. Whenever he had an issue, he found it easier to locate it when he printed it out, which made sense. He'd read studies that said people recalled things better when they were on paper.

Mia must have heard the whir of the printer. She pointed to his office and said, "Do you want me to get that?"

He nodded. "Please."

Pulling up the results from the cell phones, he once

again wondered at the overlap between the places where his brother had made calls and the calls the killer had made.

Had the killer been following his brother, or was it just happenstance that their paths had crossed?

Mia returned and sat next to him, the report in hand. Seeing that he'd paused on the results rather than recreating their street view, she said, "What's worrying you?"

He gestured to the intersecting areas of red and green circles. "I can understand that last connection. It's right before we were attacked at the office so I'm assuming he and Miles talked or texted. But these other two?"

"Maybe one is where Miles dropped off the money?" Mia said offhandedly while skimming through the report he'd printed.

"Maybe," he said and pulled up the street view for the second location they'd examined the day before. As he swiveled the view around and around, he saw it. A used-car lot just behind the bus stop.

"Is that it?" Mia asked, but even while she did so, she was perusing the list of family members. Suddenly she stopped and jabbed a finger on one of the entries.

"One of the Cruz cousins owns a used-car lot in Little Havana. Could it possibly be that one?" she said and pointed to the screen.

"Let's get the exact location," he said, then switched to a map view to get the address and read it off.

"That's it. Cruz owns that used-car lot," Mia said, excitement ringing in her voice.

Maybe that's why the thought of cars had settled into his brain much the same way a troublesome piece of code would sometimes do. The pain in his head popped like a balloon that had been overinflated, bringing welcome relief. And with that came another thought.

"Looks like we're going to buy a car."

IN THE HOPE of not being recognized, Mia had pulled her hair into a ponytail, slipped on a baseball cap from John's prodigious collection and added sunglasses.

"You look…like Mia," John said with a chuckle as they pulled out of his driveway for the trip to the used-car lot in Little Havana.

"And not one of 'the Twins,'" she said with a shake of her head.

"Not one of 'the Twins.' This you…" he said and eyed her up and down. "I like this you, but I like the other you, too. Actually, I like all the different yous."

She grinned, appreciating his honesty. He'd never treated her as a trophy, but as a real person. She realized then that she had treated him much the same way, more interested in John the man instead of the reclusive multimillionaire.

"I like the different yous, too," she teased back, but even as she did, she pulled down the visor to keep an eye on the road behind them and kept her head on a swivel to make sure they weren't being followed.

John was vigilant as well, constantly checking the road, mindful of the danger of being tracked by whoever wanted them dead.

They traveled along the A1A until they slipped onto the highway and finally pulled off onto the side streets to head to the location they had identified from the street view. When they pulled into the parking area for the business and stepped out of the car, a thirtysomething man stepped out of a building on the lot.

Victor Cruz was dressed like many Miami Cubans in a pale blue *guayabera* shirt and dark dress pants. Smiling as he saw them, he greeted them when he approached.

"Good morning. How can I help you today?" Victor said.

"My wife and I are looking for a second car," John said.

Mia added, "Nothing fancy. Just something to run errands."

"Sedan? SUV? Truck?" Victor asked.

"Truck," John said at the same time that Mia said, "Sedan."

Victor laughed and nodded. "Sedan it is. Come this way," he said and guided them in the direction of the building.

As they neared, Mia realized that the building housed not only an office area in the front, but also what looked like a repair area in the back.

"Do you fix cars also?" she asked and gestured toward the open garage doors. When they got closer, she could see there were two bays, and a car was up on a lift while a mechanic worked beside the car.

"We do. We offer a limited warranty and if anything happens during that time, we'll take care of it for you," he said and waved his hand in the direction of a long row of late-model sedans.

She and John strolled up and down the row, chatting while Victor extolled the virtues of some of the cars. She felt guilty wasting his time because they had no interest in buying a car.

Hemming and hawing, giving one excuse after another, they delayed, trying to get a feel not just for Victor, but whoever else might be at the location. As they did, she noticed that the trucks were a few rows back and much closer to the garage area, where the mechanic was still at work and where a second man had joined him.

"I know you wanted a truck, *amorcito*. Let's take a look at those," she said, then slipped her arm through John's and dragged him in the direction of the larger vehicles.

"Of course, *mi amor*. Anything for you," he said.

"Lucky man," Victor said and when she glanced over her shoulder, she caught the salesman leering at her backside.

Anger rose up, but she tamped it down and approached the row of trucks. She intentionally moved them toward the trucks closest to the garage and as they got there, the mechanic she'd noticed earlier stepped into view.

She was sure he was one of the Cruz gang-member cousins and as the man saw them, his eyes widened and to her surprise, he raced off down the side of the lot.

"He's in a hurry," she said, drawing Victor's attention to Cruz's retreating back.

Victor waved her off. "Ignore him. He's a little *loco*, but a good guy."

Not *loco* but someone who clearly knew who they were and didn't want to stick around.

When she met John's gaze, he'd realized the same thing.

They hurried off, saying they had to think about it, hopped in the car and circled around to go in the direction they'd seen Cruz take off. While they did that, Mia called Trey, who immediately conferenced in Roni.

"That was a risky thing to do," she said while the sounds of station-house activity filtered across the line.

"We had a hunch. The lot belongs to Victor Cruz, one of the cousins," Mia explained.

"Stay put. Roni will meet you there with backup," Trey said.

"He's already on the run. We're trying to track him down," Mia said, craning her head every which way to see where Cruz may have gone, but it was no use. Behind the car lot were a number of stores, and he could have easily slipped into one or found a hiding place in any of the alleys.

"Go back to the location and wait for me. In the meantime, I just sent Sophie and Robbie the ATM footage from both of those banks. Hopefully they can find something," Roni said and hung up.

Mia looked at him, but he had heard the conversation. "The risk was worth it," he said and steered back toward Cruz's car lot, but parked on the street to wait for Roni.

"It was. If he ran it's because he recognized us and knew why we were there," she said in agreement while they waited.

It didn't take more than about twenty minutes for Roni to pull up in a nondescript sedan with her partner.

Mia and John left their car to meet them, and Roni introduced her partner. "Detective Heath Williams. Meet John Wilson. I think you already know Mia."

"I do," he said with a smile and held out his hand to John. Williams was a good-looking man who seemed better-suited to a modeling gig than being a cop. Just over six foot, he had a lean muscular build, ice-blue eyes, boyish dimples and hair the color of chestnuts. She'd dated him once, and once had been more than enough, but he was a good cop.

"Hang back while Heath and I speak to Cruz," she said.

Roni was in cop mode and Mia always marveled at all the different roles her best friend seemed to handle with such ease. Today she was dressed in her black suit and was all business, but she'd seen Roni dressed to the nines for undercover work and totally casual when she hung out with the family.

As they strolled toward the building, Roni and Williams looked around, taking in the location.

Cruz must have seen them coming since he hurried out of the office area to greet them.

He looked from Roni and Williams to them, brow furrowed with puzzlement. "Officers. Mr. and Mrs... I never did get your names."

"John Wilson and Mia Gonzalez," John said, gesturing between the two of them.

Victor clapped his hands and laughed, seemingly unperturbed by the presence of the police. "I knew I recognized you even with the disguise."

"Mr. Cruz. We need to ask you some questions," Roni said.

He seemed startled by her tone, as if finally realizing that this was serious. "Sure. Come into the office," he said, inviting them in with a sweep of his hand.

Roni jerked her head in Williams's direction, instructing him to hang back by the door while they entered.

Inside, Victor went to a desk and sat, but the three of them stood there while Roni began her interrogation.

"I understand that your cousin Alejandro Cruz works for you," Roni said.

Victor flipped a hand in the direction of her and John. "Like I told them, there's no need to worry about him."

"I ran his record on the way over. Breaking and entering. Assault and battery. Seems like a reasonable person might be worried about having someone like that around," Roni pressed.

Victor raised his hands for understanding. "He's family. I couldn't say no even if he has problems."

"Has problems? Want to explain?" Roni said.

Victor circled an index finger around his temple. "He thinks he and his friends are going to invade Cuba someday and set it free. Be just like our *abuelo*, who took part in the Bay of Pigs."

Roni looked over her shoulder at them, eyes wide in disbelief, before she schooled her features and returned her attention to Cruz.

"How do they plan to do that?" she asked, a too calm chill in her voice.

For the first time since they'd gotten there, Victor started to fidget. He picked up a pen from his desk and flipped it from end to end. "It's nothing serious. Just a couple of guys on the weekends. Camping and stuff."

"Stuff. What kinds of stuff?" Roni pressed.

"It's a free country, *sabes*. They're not doing anything illegal," he said, but the flipping of the pen got faster and faster.

Roni reached out and stopped him. "Why don't you let me be the judge of that?"

Victor eyeballed Roni and then them. With a shake of his head, he said, "I'm not the guy to tell you." He grabbed a piece of paper and wrote something down. Handed the paper to Roni. "Sam Hidalgo is the head of the group. They call themselves the Cuban Democratic Army. He'll be able to tell you more."

"Thanks," Roni said and began to turn away. But

then she faced Cruz again and said, "If your cousin comes back, play it cool and call us." She took a business card from her pocket and handed it to him.

With a tip of her head, Roni instructed them to exit the office.

Mia went first, with Roni following and finally John. They met Williams, who jerked his chin up in question. "Get anything?"

Roni waved the piece of paper with the name and number. As she did so, a trio of chirps sounded from their phones.

Almost in unison they whipped out their phones to review the message they'd just received.

The message was from Trey and as Mia pulled up the short video, she gasped.

Chapter Twenty-One

"That's him," Mia said on a shocked breath.

John paused the video and zoomed in as a man bumped into Miles, seemingly accidentally, only they all knew there had been nothing accidental about it.

"That's Alejandro Cruz," John said and shook his head. "That's when he must have put the tracker on Miles."

"That cinches it. We have reasonable cause for a BOLO," Roni said, and Williams nodded in agreement.

"What about the group? What do you do about that?" John asked.

Roni smiled harshly. "If it's one of the 500 or more militias scattered across the US, we should probably check with the Feds before we do anything."

Williams nodded. "We don't want to step on one of their investigations."

"500 or more?" Mia almost croaked.

"That's actually down from the over 600 in 2018," Roni said with a shake of her head.

"What do we do now?" John asked, worried that with Cruz on the run he might be even more deadly.

"Go home and stay home. A cornered animal can be dangerous," Roni said.

While John didn't like the idea of hiding, he also

didn't want to risk Mia's life and she and the rest of the family were Cruz's primary targets.

"We'll be there. Call us if you have any developments," John said and escorted Mia back to their car.

Once they were buckled in, he took off for home, but nervous tension filled the vehicle.

"I almost can't believe we have him," Mia said.

He couldn't believe it either. Wouldn't believe it until their attacker was behind bars. "We still need to be careful."

Come to think of it, so did Miles. "Can you do me a favor and send that video to Miles and warn him about Cruz?"

"I will," she said.

From the corner of his eye, he watched her texting away, but then he returned his attention to the road, vigilant for signs that anyone was following them. His eye caught Mia beside him, also attentive to what was happening all around. Thankfully, they arrived at his home without incident.

As soon as they walked through the door, Mia wrapped her arms around herself and said, "I can't just sit here and do nothing."

"Neither can I," he said and immediately raced to the wall safe in his bedroom, where he had locked up his laptop. He hadn't wanted to haul it with him and had secured it until their return.

When he went to the dining room, Mia was already sitting there on her laptop. "These guys—the Cuban Democratic Army—they're dangerous. Over ten years ago they were responsible for an attack in New York City that killed five FBI agents and wounded three others."

The articles that he pulled up were older, mostly around the time of the New York City attack. "Not much new information," he said, wondering if it was because most of the members had been jailed or gone into hiding.

"Nothing really, and Cruz would have been young during that big attack. Only fifteen," Mia said.

"But his older cousin was twenty and already involved with the gang. Alejandro Cruz goes from being groomed there to somehow connecting with the militia and it makes sense. He's got a beef with your family about whatever happened to his grandfather. A man he idolizes to the point he wants to be just like him and liberate Cuba."

"And the militia clearly had the capability of making bombs and training him to shoot," Mia repeated.

"The program was useless because there wasn't enough data about the militia and how Cruz was connected to it," John said with a shake of his head.

"Garbage in, garbage out," Mia said sympathetically and slipped her hand over his.

With a laugh, he said, "I'm almost relieved about that. I was so worried about this becoming something all-knowing and so dangerous."

"Enough data and it could be, but I trust you not to let it get that way," she said.

"You have a lot of faith in me," he said and twined his fingers with hers.

She smiled, her blue eyes dark, but happy despite everything that was happening. "I do because… I love you, John. It's crazy and it doesn't make any sense—"

He cut her off with a kiss because he didn't want to hear all the buts. Lord knows he'd been thinking about them from the day he'd first met her and now…

"I love you, too, Mia. You are such an amazing woman," he said. He cradled her cheek and stroked his thumb across her smooth cheek.

He was leaning in to kiss her again when his phone

chirped. He wanted to ignore it especially when he saw it was Miles, but swiped it open.

Cold filled his core at the photo of Miles tied to a chair. A bruise marred his cheek. His shirt was torn open and stained with blood.

"John? What's wrong?" Mia asked.

John held up his phone and Mia's face turned a sickly green.

"No. That's not possible. We just texted him."

But when he checked the time, he realized it had been over an hour since Cruz had run away from the lot.

Another text arrived. Call the cops and I kill him.

"We have to call Roni," Mia said.

John shook his head. "We can't. He'll kill him."

Mia laid her hand on John's. "He's going to do it either way. You know that."

Another ding. His hands shook as he read it.

I want Mia and a million dollars. Small bills.

Ten million. No Mia.

A long pause followed, but then Cruz responded. K. Tomorrow. Noon.

Where?

I'll let you know.

JOHN AND MIA sat with the family at his dining-room table, while Roni, her partner and someone who Roni had identified as FBI Agent Garcia zoomed into the call.

"Agent Garcia is familiar with the CDA. He was one

of the agents wounded during the New York City attack," Roni explained.

"Thank you for being with us, Agent Garcia. My family appreciates any help you can provide," Trey said and dipped his head in greeting.

"Thank you, Mr. Gonzalez. We've been watching the CDA for years," the agent said.

Garcia was a recklessly handsome man in his late thirties with just a hint of gray at his temples. Light green eyes were striking even via the camera.

"Why are they still in business?" Mia asked, frustrated that the dangerous group was still in existence.

The agent's lips firmed, and his gaze hardened. "The situation was complicated. We charged those we could but didn't cut the head off the snake."

"And they reorganized and survived," John said.

Roni and her partner shared a look. "Agent Garcia is not sure the CDA is behind this abduction."

"Why does that matter? Isn't kidnapping a federal crime?" Mia challenged.

"This kidnapping normally wouldn't fit the criteria for us to have jurisdiction, but since it does include a CDA member, we're willing to provide assistance," Garcia said.

Mia was about to lose her temper, but Trey gently squeezed her hand. "We will get the help we need, *hermanita.*"

"We're determining the location of the call and we have an inside man who might be able to provide more info," Garcia advised.

"What do we do next?" John asked, worry etching deep lines onto his face.

"He'll be watching, so we'll need to be careful," Garcia advised.

"I'm ready. Whatever you need," John said with no hesitation.

Mia wished she could be as sure. Fear twisted her guts into knots and it didn't unravel as the video call ended and her family rallied around them.

"It's going to be okay," Sophie reassured her, but Mia wasn't an idiot. It was impossible to miss the worry on the faces of her family as they sat around the table.

"The FBI will provide everything they have on the militia. We'll process it and devise our own plan, just in case," Trey said.

"We will," Robbie chimed in.

Mia forced a smile and glanced at John from the corner of her eye. His face reflected what she was feeling, but she put a brave face on for him.

"It'll be okay. We're family and we take care of family," she said.

Mia paced back and forth and waved her arms wildly. "Why do you have to do this?"

"It's what he instructed," John said as Trey adjusted the straps on the bulletproof vest. "Should it be so tight?" he asked.

Trey tugged on the bottom. "We have to make sure it covers all the vital spots."

"Vital spots! Is it going to stop a head shot?" Mia nearly screamed.

John met Trey's gaze and the other man left the bedroom. John walked over to Mia and slipped his arms around her.

"It's going to be all right. The FBI has a team ready—"

"But they can't plan for every contingency," she said as tears glistened in her gaze.

"Is this my kick-ass warrior? The woman who can handle anything—"

"Except watching you have your head blown off," Mia challenged, but she was calmer than before.

"Which won't happen," he said, and they walked out of the bedroom to where Trey stood with FBI Agent Garcia.

Garcia handed him an earpiece. "We need to do a sound check."

John slipped it in and nodded. "I'm ready."

"Everyone check in," Garcia said, and, in his ear, John heard the various agents in and around the Bay of Pigs Monument confirm they were in position.

He nodded to acknowledge that he'd heard, and Garcia said, "Good. You remember what to do?"

The texts from Cruz with the directions had been straightforward. "Bag with the money goes in front of the monument."

Garcia handed him the reusable grocery bag from a local store. Cruz had insisted on that and the FBI had filled the bag with bundles of counterfeit hundreds.

"Leave it and walk away. As soon as you do, we'll move in as well as raid the CDA location where we believe Miles is being held," he said.

"Are you sure about that?" Trey asked. He'd been standing off to the side, arms tucked across his chest, Mia beside him.

"We're pretty sure. Our inside man identified it as a shack the CDA has on the outskirts of the Everglades," Garcia said and peered at his watch. "Time to go."

John nodded but took a quick second to hug Mia. He whispered in her ear, "Don't worry."

He glanced at Trey, silently begging him to take care of her and his friend nodded.

His friend, he thought. If this was going to be it, he could at least say that he had friends, even family, who cared about him.

Grabbing the bag, he stepped out of the home the FBI was using for the operation. It was a short distance to the corner, and he turned onto *Calle Ocho* in the direction of the memorial honoring the heroes of the invasion.

Head on a swivel, he looked around for Cruz. Nothing. Just typical lunch-hour traffic at the fast-food chicken place and strip mall across the way. He crossed over to a small local supermarket—the one that gave out reusable bags just like the one holding the ransom money.

On the other side of *Calle Ocho* was a black hexagonal column honoring the Bay of Pigs martyrs. The column sat on two hexagonal tiers of black and was surrounded by chains. He crossed the street and placed the bag in front of the monument, as he'd been instructed.

But he hadn't taken more than a step or two when a commotion across the street made him stop. Suddenly, nearly a dozen women, all carrying the same reusable shopping bags as he'd laid at the monument, streamed out of the supermarket and headed in the direction of the square.

"Keep your eyes on that drop. Keep moving, Wilson," Garcia instructed over the earpiece.

He wanted to hang back, wanted to see if Cruz was somehow in that gaggle of women, but he did as he was told and walked up *Calle Ocho*. He wondered if at the far end, which ran deep in the Everglades, the agents had been able to rescue Miles.

"I think I see him," Garcia said over the earpiece.

He headed back toward the supermarket and the

home where Trey and Mia were waiting with Garcia for word that Cruz had been apprehended.

"Tracker says he's on the path toward the next memorial," one agent said.

He faced SW 13th Street, where some of the women were also strolling down the island in the middle of the street. But suddenly a quartet of agents streamed in, and the women scattered like pigeons in a park chased away by a determined dog.

It happened so fast it almost didn't seem real. One second there was what appeared to be an older woman standing there, but then she was suddenly on the ground. When two of the agents hauled her to her feet, the wig flew off.

Cruz.

It's over, he thought, relief washing over him.

As the agents walked Cruz toward the street, an unmarked FBI sedan pulled up.

John stood there watching. Barely a few minutes later, Mia was wrapping her arms around him.

"See, head still intact," he teased, but her body jumped beside his as something punched into his side.

Two agents rushed off in the direction of a nearby strip mall and opened fire on a car that was parked there. Glancing across the street, Cruz smiled at him before the FBI agents hurriedly stuffed him into the sedan.

As Mia's knees folded, he gently lowered her to the ground, in disbelief at the sight of the blood seeping from her side. Garcia's frantic calls in his ear, screaming for an ambulance.

"Mia," he said as he cradled her, but she'd passed out.

Trey kneeled at his side, shock on his face, then he went into action, ripping off his shirt and tearing it in half. He wadded the fabric and said, "Apply pressure."

Apply pressure, he thought, thinking this couldn't be real. But the warmth of her blood against his hand was only too real.

He placed one wad at her back while Trey took the other and applied it to the exit wound. She moaned, bringing joy because that meant she was still alive.

The wail of the ambulance filled his ears as it screeched to a stop.

EMTs jumped from the vehicle and took over, moving Mia onto a gurney and loading her into the ambulance. He stood there, her blood drying on his hands, as the ambulance raced away.

Garcia approached, his face somber. "We should have seen that coming."

"We should have," Trey chimed in, shoulders slumped. His voice was filled with guilt and…defeat.

"She'll be fine," he said to convince Trey and himself.

Barely a breath left him before Garcia's phone chirped. The agent answered and his mood stayed stoic.

John's heart pounded in his ears, so loudly he didn't hear what Garcia had said. It was Trey who repeated it and he finally understood.

"They have Miles and he's okay."

Okay. Miles was okay, but as he peered at his hands, the blood there warned that nothing was okay and might not ever be again.

JOHN SAT BESIDE Mia's bed, holding her hand. Tubes and wires ran from her to assorted monitors that beeped and blinked with signs of life while Mia lay uncomfortably still.

Complications during surgery. Coma.

The words kept on repeating in his brain throughout

the night and into the morning, but nothing changed except for the ebb and flow of the Gonzalez family members coming and going from the room.

He left her side only to relieve himself and grab a candy bar, stale and tasteless, from one of the hospital vending machines.

"You need to go get some rest," Trey said and laid a hand on his shoulder.

Looking up at his friend, John wondered if he looked as bad. Smudges dark as bruises sat below his aqua-colored eyes. He obviously hadn't been getting any rest when he wasn't at the hospital.

"We'll stay with her," Roni said. She was tucked into her fiancée's side, offering support.

"I'm not leaving."

Realizing that he wouldn't budge, Roni said, "I'm going to get you something to eat."

With a kiss on Trey's cheek, she hurried from the room and Trey almost toppled into a chair that protested his weight with a worrisome creak. "She's going to pull through this," he said, but his voice lacked the usual confidence he had come to expect from Trey.

He wanted to believe it even as frustration at being helpless made him clench his fists. "I wish there was more we could do."

Trey bowed at the waist and leaned his forearms on his thighs. "They say people in comas can hear what you say."

With a shrug and a shake of his head, he wondered what he could possibly say besides that he loved her. He was grateful he'd already told her before…

"You were always trying to pry it out of me, so here goes."

At Trey's puzzled look, he explained. "She wanted to

know more about me. About where I came from. Things like that."

"As good a thing as any to tell her," Trey said with a tired smile. He sat back in his chair, prepared to listen as well.

Normally John wouldn't share such personal things with strangers. But Trey wasn't a stranger. He was a friend, but more importantly, he was family now.

"I was born in Lancaster County. My dad's family settled there in the early 1800s, but my dad lost the farm when I was six and we moved to Philly," he began. He talked until Roni came back with a sandwich and soda for him.

Trey took over, sharing a story about when he'd tried to cut a wad of gum out of her hair and nearly scalped her, and another time when Ricky and he had embarrassed her when they'd found her necking with a boyfriend at the movie theater.

Roni chimed in, regaling them with a tale about their antics at a college frat party.

He finished his sandwich and resumed his position at Mia's bedside, sharing bits and pieces from his past, tag-teaming with other family members until night came again.

This time it was her father who urged him to go.

"Samantha and I can do the night shift," Ramon said and jerked his head in the direction of Mia's mom as she entered.

"I'm not leaving," he said, but gave her parents space so Mia would know they were there.

They left around midnight, and he resumed his vigil, softly sharing his life with her until his voice was hoarse, his throat sore, but the pain didn't silence him. Sleep claimed him in the early morning hours.

Her voice drifted into his dreams. "Philly?" she said.

Philly? he thought and jerked awake when he heard it again.

Mia's eyes fluttered open, and she grimaced. "Hurts."

"I'll call the nurse," he said, but she grabbed hold of his hand.

"No. Okay. Philly? Really?" she said, her words clipped as if each one brought pain.

"You heard me?" he asked, thinking back to when he'd been sharing with her. He didn't recall any moment when she'd seemed lucid.

She nodded. "I heard. I love a guy from Philly," she said, slightly stronger and with a shadow of a smile.

"And I love you, Mia. I don't want to spend another moment without you," he said and gently leaned over to press a tender kiss on her temple.

"I'm not going anywhere without you," she said, and her smile strengthened.

"No, you're not."

Epilogue

Why have only one wedding when it was just as easy to have two? Mia thought. Especially since she and Roni were best friends and would have the same bridal parties and guests.

Mia watched Roni walk down the aisle to meet Trey at the altar of the cathedral. The organist paused and started the wedding march again.

"Are you ready, *mi'ja*?" her father asked and slipped his arm through hers.

She nodded. "Never more ready, *Papi*."

Together they marched down the aisle to where John waited for her along with the rest of the bridal party. Sophie, Carolina and Mariela wore gowns in a pale shade of coral. Opposite them, Ricky, Robbie and Miles stood handsomely in white dinner jackets, black pants and coral bow ties and pocket squares.

She had been surprised when John had asked about having Miles in the bridal party, but since the kidnapping, the brothers seemed to have reconciled to some extent.

John, she thought with a loving sigh and met his gaze down what seemed the too long length of the aisle.

He stood beside Trey—both of them were breathtakingly handsome in their dinner jackets. Roni was already at Trey's side, waiting for her best friend.

Mia quickened her pace, earning a hushed *"Cálmate."*

Sucking in a breath, she calmed herself and her pace until she reached him.

He seemed just as anxious, since he stepped down from the altar to take her hand even before her father could hand her to him.

It prompted laughter from everyone around them, but she didn't care.

He was nothing like what some might call the perfect man, but he was the perfect man for her.

"I love you," he whispered and guided her to her spot on the altar.

JOHN HELD HER hand tightly, almost not believing that they were here. That they were getting married.

It had been weeks since she'd been shot, but he'd been with her every step of the way, sharing his Indian Creek home with her as she'd slowly healed. Sharing the bits and pieces of his past as they built their future together. Even the painful past about his father and his mother's death and the fresh pain of his brother's betrayal.

He shot a quick look over at his brother. They'd had a reckoning, the two of them, about what Miles's role might be in John's new life. Miles had understood.

They'd always be brothers, but nothing else. John wasn't sure he could ever truly trust him again.

Unlike the woman beside him. Brave, intelligent, caring. Strong, so strong.

She was the kind of woman any man would be lucky

to have in their life. A life that included her amazing family as well.

Mia squeezed his hand tight, yanking him from his thoughts. She tilted her head in the direction of the priest, who repeated, "Do you, John Xavier Wilson—"

"I do," he interrupted, eliciting waves of laughter again from everyone in the church.

The priest shook his head, chuckled and glanced at Mia. "Do you—"

"I do," she answered, and he knew everything was going to be more than okay.

It was going to be perfect.

* * * * *

*Don't miss more South Beach Security books,
this time featuring K-9s, coming soon from
New York Times bestselling author
Caridad Piñeiro!*

*And if you missed the previous books in
Caridad Piñeiro's South Beach Security miniseries,
look for:*

Lost in Little Havana
Brickell Avenue Ambush

*Available now wherever Harlequin Intrigue
books are sold!*